ON THE WAY TO SAN JOSE

Jere' M. Fishback

Terrence, a socially inept clarinetist whose driver's license is suspended, needs his panel van driven from Orlando to San Jose, where he plans to start a new life. Levi's a Stanford University student with Asperger's Syndrome who answers Terrence's Internet drive-away listing.

The two start out as strangers, but as their journey westward progresses a friendship is kindled, one that will change both boys' lives in profound ways.

Published by
NineStar Press
PO Box 91792
Albuquerque, New Mexico, 87199
www.ninestarpress.com

Warning: This book contains sexual content, which is only suitable for mature readers.

Print ISBN #978-1-947139-94-7
Cover by Natasha Snow
Edited by Jason Bradley

Chapter One

LEVI MCKANE STUDIED an Internet drive-away listing:

Need vehicle driven from Orlando to San Jose, CA. We can split the gas. I want to leave ASAP.

The listing provided a phone number.

Levi was twenty with an athletic build, cobalt eyes, and sandy hair that grew to his shoulders. He would start his third year at Stanford University in two weeks. He'd earned himself a full academic scholarship to the California school after graduating second in his class from Merritt Island High in Brevard County, Florida two years before.

But his life was not perfect.

When Levi was four years old, a child development specialist diagnosed him with a mild form of Asperger's Syndrome, a disorder causing difficulties in social interaction. So, despite his high intelligence, Levi had never mastered the art of human communication. At school and home, he said little. He kept to himself and avoided eye contact. Conversations, even with family members, seemed like thickets to Levi. He had no close friends in either Brevard County or California, and until recently had never dated. In truth, he felt the happiest fishing by himself on his parents' dock with a six-pack of beer at his side.

"Leave him alone," his dad must have told Levi's mother a thousand times. "It won't be long before he figures himself out."

Over summer break from Stanford, Levi had saved up three thousand dollars while working at his dad's auto repair business on Merritt Island. He could have flown to California if he chose to, but didn't want to waste part of his summer earnings on airfare, not with the problem he faced.

He'd met a girl named Taylor back in June. She waited tables at a beachfront grill that Levi sometimes patronized after surfing at the Cocoa Beach Pier. Taylor wasn't the subtle type; right away she let Levi know she liked him. And Levi, being a socially artless boy, let her take him down a path he hadn't walked before. One thing led to another, and now Taylor was pregnant.

While he studied his computer screen, Levi thought of the phone call he'd received from Taylor a month before: "As of yesterday, I was late on my period two weeks. I knew something was wrong, so I bought a testing kit, and now it's for certain. What'll we do?"

"We?" Levi said. "Are you even sure it's mine?"

"Positive, *asshole.*"

They discussed abortion. Taylor wasn't inclined, as she was Catholic. Then they discussed marriage. Levi wasn't inclined, as he was due back at Stanford. And though he didn't tell her so, Taylor wasn't exactly someone he'd want to share life with. A girl of limited intellect and shrill voice, she was rough around the edges, and Levi knew she'd wear the pants in whatever marriage she made—a union he wanted no part of.

So, the pregnancy floated in limbo.

Levi studied the Internet offer again. He had drive-away experience. At the end of last school year, he'd driven a retiree's Crown Victoria from San Francisco to St. Petersburg. The old guy even kicked in two hundred bucks for gasoline. Levi made the cross-country trip in five days and delivered the car to the owner's Florida condo where Levi's mom picked him up and drove him to Florida's east coast.

Making the three thousand mile trip by himself had not bothered him. He liked listening to the Crown Vic's radio while traversing the never-ending brownness of southern Arizona and New Mexico, and then the ceaseless hill country of west Texas. The whole experience made him feel like the characters in one of his favorite books, *On The Road* by Jack Kerouac.

Now, seated at his parents' kitchen table, Levi swung his gaze to a pair of double-hung windows with a view of the Indian River. He scratched his chin stubble while watching a shrimp boat cruise past his family's dock, likely headed to Sebastian Inlet. The boat's gauzy nets fluttered like dragonfly wings. Sunlight reflected in the boat's wake that ruffled the river's otherwise glassy surface. The time was close to 9:00 a.m. and already the day was heating up. By noon, the temperature would hit ninety-two; the relative humidity would likely reach a similar level, and Levi was glad he wasn't working at the garage that day. He could stay in the air-conditioned comfort of his parents' home.

When Levi punched up the phone number in the drive-away ad, a boy answered on the second ring, his voice a scratchy tenor. He answered Levi's questions in a rapid-fire cadence, as though he couldn't get the words out of his mouth fast enough.

"It's actually a van, not a car."

"No, it doesn't have air-conditioning."

"Yeah, I'd be riding with you to San Jose. I can't drive; my license is suspended."

When the boy asked Levi how soon he could make the trip, Levi said, "I can leave the day after tomorrow. I'll still need to pack my things."

They talked money.

"The whole trip's 2,800 miles," the boy said. "The van gets twenty miles per gallon on the road, so we'll burn about three hundred dollars' worth of gas. And then we'll need to rent motel rooms for at least four or five nights, so I figure—"

"I don't do motels," Levi interjected. "I tent camp in parks and cook my own meals on a propane stove; it saves a lot of money."

The boy was silent for a moment. Then he said, "I guess I could sleep in the van, but I don't really know how to cook."

"We can split the cost of food," Levi said. "I'll cook and you can clean up afterward; how's that?"

More silence, this time for about thirty seconds.

"Are you still there?" Levi said.

"Yeah," the boy replied, "I'm just thinking."

"About what?"

"Are you somebody I can trust? I mean, I've never done this before. How do I know you're not some kind of psycho?"

Levi drew a breath and then let it out while he fingered the edge of his cell phone. "I go to college in northern California. I can show you my university ID. And I'm a good driver—I've never had a ticket—so you don't have to worry about me. I'll get you and your van there safely."

They traded names and e-mail addresses. The boy's name was Terrence DeVine; he lived in east Orlando, not far from the Orange Blossom Trail.

"I'm moving to San Jose," he said, "to live with a friend."

They agreed Levi's mom could drop him off at Terrence's house at 9:00 a.m. two days hence, a Thursday. "We can hit the road as soon as I load up my stuff," Levi said. "We should make it to Alabama by dinnertime."

"Sounds good," Terrence said. "I'll see you then."

LEVI AND TAYLOR faced each other in a booth at Taco City in south Cocoa Beach, just a mile from Patrick Air Force Base, where Taylor's dad served. The restaurant was a Brevard County institution; it served tasty Mexican cuisine and draft beer so cold it numbed the back of your throat on the first swallow. The crowd that night was a mix of surfers, condo dwellers, young families with kids in high chairs, and servicemen sporting crew cuts.

Taylor looked nice enough in her short shorts and a tank top. Her straight brown hair was parted in the middle; it draped her shoulders. Her dark eyes focused on Levi while she toyed with her uneaten burrito.

"This is *both* our responsibilities," she said. "I can't believe you're running off to California while I'm stuck here with this...situation."

Levi lowered his gaze and rubbed his lips together while his brain churned. Why hadn't he used a condom? He'd never even asked Taylor if she was on the pill before they started having sex. He'd just assumed as much, and how stupid was that?

"I'm on scholarship," he told Taylor. "I can't just not show up."

Taylor glanced here and there. Then she said, "You could enroll at UCF's campus in Cocoa. At least that way you'd be here when the baby arrives in April."

Levi shook his head. "It's not going to happen."

"Why?"

"Stanford's one of the best schools in the country. I won't walk away from there just because you're pregnant."

Taylor squirmed on her bench while she twirled a strand of her hair around a finger. "You're dumping this whole thing on me, you know, and it's not fair."

Levi wasn't in the mood to argue, so he didn't respond to Taylor's last remark. Instead, he told her, "I'm leaving tomorrow, but I'll call you from the road Friday night. Think again about an abortion; I'll pay half."

Taylor didn't say anything; she only stared out a window at traffic passing on A-1-A.

Chapter Two

TERRENCE'S HOUSE LOOKED much like all the others in its neighborhood, a single-story cinder-block structure with a one-car garage, an asphalt shingle roof, and casement windows that opened like book covers. Spindly azalea bushes clung to the walls, and a pair of tired-looking foxtail palms grew in the Bahia grass yard. A real estate agent's sign said the sale of the property was pending. A bathtub Madonna stood on the home's open front porch next to an aluminum lawn chair with shredded webbing.

A panel van, easily a dozen years old, sat in the driveway. The name of a company, Bo Peep Dry Cleaners, adorned both the van's flanks along with silhouettes of a little girl in a frilly dress who balanced an open parasol on her shoulder. The van's bumpers were dented, its paint job was chalky, and one of the rear windows was cracked.

When Levi tried ringing the home's doorbell, it didn't produce sound, so Levi rapped on the frame of the jalousie front door instead. Then he shifted his weight from one leg to the other while he studied a cobweb in one corner of the porch ceiling.

A slender boy with delicate facial features answered the door. Dressed in a faded polo shirt, khaki shorts, and high-top Converse sneakers with no socks, he was half a head shorter than Levi. His dark hair grew over his ears and his cola-colored eyes wiggled in their sockets when his gaze met Levi's.

"Hey," he said. "I'm Terrence."

The two shook hands and then Levi pointed to the van. "Is that our ride?"

Terrence nodded.

Levi made a face like he'd swallowed a shot of lemon juice. "Are you sure that thing will *make* it to California?"

Terrence's cheeks colored while he brushed his bangs from his forehead. "I had it checked out by a mechanic. He said everything's working fine."

"All right, then," Levi said. "Let me get my stuff, and then we can go."

Levi and his mom went about transferring Levi's possessions to the van while Terrence went back inside his house. There wasn't all that much to load up: a few boxes of clothing and shoes, a laptop computer bag, Levi's tent and sleeping bag, his cook stove and ice cooler, and a box containing a clutter of cooking paraphernalia.

The van's interior was entirely unfinished, save for the driver and passenger seats up front. Levi studied the van's ribbed steel floor and buttressed steel walls that were dented and scratched from years of use. Several cardboard boxes were stacked against one wall, each cross-flapped and labeled with a felt-tipped pen: "clothes," "shoes," books," "games," and so forth. An object resembling a small suitcase with aluminum trim and twin hasp fasteners rested on top of one box.

The day was heating up—so was the van—and Levi shook his head when he recalled that the van was not air-conditioned. Already his shirt stuck to the small of his back.

When the loading process was finished, Levi hugged his teary-eyed mom and gave her a kiss goodbye. "I'll call you tonight from Alabama," he said, and then he waved to her from the curb as he watched her drive away. Like always, he felt conflicted about putting three thousand miles between himself and his parents. But during his past two years of college, the space between Florida and California had given Levi a sense of freedom like he'd never known before. Nobody made decisions for him in Palo Alto. No one looked over his shoulder or offered him unsolicited advice, and no one tried to force conversations on him.

He liked all of that very much.

The hinges on Terrence's front door squeaked, causing Levi to turn just as Terrence emerged from his house with a pillow under one arm and a rolled-up sleeping bag under the other. The bag was bright pink, with a motif of purple and yellow poodles scattered across it.

When Terrence approached, Levi winced and pointed at the bag. "What *is* that?"

Terrence looked at the bag, then at Levi. "I'll need it if I'm sleeping in the van."

Levi shook his head. "It's awfully *colorful*."

Terrence shrugged. Then he pointed to the sign on the van's flank. "My grandpa owns Bo Peep. A customer left the bag to be dry-cleaned and then they never came back for it. Why should I buy a bag when I can use this one for free?"

A gray-haired woman in a housedress and slippers emerged from Terrence's house with a flannel bathrobe draped over her arm. "Terry, don't forget this," she cried out from the porch. "The weather gets cold in California."

Terrence looked at the woman while he let out his breath. "All right, Grandma," he said with a tone of resignation in his voice, "I'll take it along." After he strode to the porch, he slung the robe over a shoulder while the woman prattled.

"Don't pick up hitchhikers; you never know who they might be. And be sure to take your multivitamin in the morning. I put extra jelly on your sandwich, just as you like it. And don't forget to call us each night to let us know where you're at."

"Okay, Grandma, *okay*...."

After Terrence hugged the woman goodbye, he returned to the driveway where he handed Levi a key chain with a Mickey Mouse medallion hanging from it. "Ready to go?"

Levi nodded, and moments later, the van's engine roared to life. Terrence waved at his grandmother as Levi backed the van into the street. Then, after they drove off, Terrence pulled a creased and coffee-stained roadmap from the van's glove box.

"Hang a left at the next intersection," he told Levi, and then he pointed to the map he held. "I studied this last night. Our best route is taking Highway 50 to the Florida Turnpike. Then we'll take the turnpike north to I-75."

Levi shook his head. "Who needs maps? Use the GPS on your phone."

"My phone doesn't *have* a GPS," Terrence said.

"Sure it does," Levi said while holding out his hand. "Let me see it."

Terrence fumbled in his pocket for a moment before producing a mobile phone identical to one Levi's dad had owned when Levi was ten years old.

After Terrence handed the phone to Levi, he said, "I can talk and text on it, but that's all."

Levi studied the phone while he shook his head. "Why don't you upgrade?"

Terrence shrugged but didn't say anything when Levi handed the phone back. Instead, after Terrence pocketed the phone, he studied his road map again. "The intersection with 50 should come up in just a few miles. Take a right when we get there."

"I don't *need* directions," Levi said while he stared out the windshield. Then he pulled out his smart phone and held it up for Terrence to see. "I'm living in the twenty-first century."

Terrence lowered his gaze without saying anything in response. Then they rode in silence for a spell, which suited Levi just fine.

Traffic on Highway 50, also known as Colonial Drive, was a hodgepodge of transfer trucks, city buses, taxi cabs, dump trucks, and private vehicles. Levi and Terrence passed used car dealerships, gas station/convenience stores, strip malls, fast food restaurants, and shopping centers where half the storefronts were empty. The entire area was devoid of trees and shrubs; it seemed to Levi that decades ago the area's developers had bulldozed any flora that had once grown there. The air smelled like a mixture of diesel fumes, burnt rubber, and fried food.

Levi shook his head while he studied his surroundings. He had never liked Orlando with its endless sprawl of subdivisions, outlet malls, tourist hotels, and theme parks. The whole city had an impersonal and temporary feel to it, as though most buildings he saw, even the newer ones, would likely not be there in thirty years. Why would people choose to live in such a place?

But the farther west they drove, the less congested things became. They crossed Lake Sherwood and then Lake Lotta. They passed by gated subdivisions and even a few cattle ranches. Levi felt himself relax a little as they left the city behind them. Once on the turnpike, they cruised at a speed of seventy miles per hour. The engine hummed, and Levi noticed how the van's heavy suspension allowed for a smooth ride.

Both Levi and Terrence had their windows lowered. Warm air rushed through the van; it tossed Terrence's hair about as he stared out the windshield and rubbed the tip of his nose with a knuckle.

"So, what's California like?"

Levi looked at Terrence and furrowed his brow. "You've never been?"

Terrence shook his head. "I've never gone outside of Florida."

Levi returned his gaze to the road. In front of them, a dump truck with a ragged canvas cover kept pelting the van's windshield with sand. "Most of southern California is ugly and crowded. But northern California is sweet, especially if you enjoy the outdoors. Does your friend like to camp and hike?"

Terrence crinkled his forehead. "What friend?"

"The one you're going to live with."

"Oh...him. I don't really know; I haven't asked."

Levi puckered one side of his face when he looked at Terrence. "How long have you known this guy?"

Terrence shrugged. "A few months; we met over the Internet."

"So you've never talked to him in person?"

"Nope."

Levi shook his head while he steered the van into the fast lane. Then he punched the accelerator. Within seconds, they had passed the dump truck, and then Levi returned the van to the outside lane.

Terrence chewed a hangnail while he stared out the windshield. They passed the southern shore of Lake Apopka, an enormous expanse of water, and then the turnpike's surrounding landscape became entirely rural: forest, orange groves, tomato fields, and cattle farms. The flatness of central Florida gave way to a more uneven terrain. Neither boy said a word for a half hour or more until Terrence asked who Levi would live with when they reached California.

"Since I'm a junior this year, I'll have my own apartment on campus; it's an efficiency with a kitchen and everything. It'll be *so* much better than the dorm I lived in before."

"Is the rent high?" Terrence asked.

"Like I told you," Levi said, "I'm on scholarship, so I don't pay anything."

Terrence rearranged his limbs. "What kind of stuff do you study?"

"I'm majoring in Forestry, so I take mostly science and agriculture courses. What about you? Taken any college classes?"

Terrence shook his head. "I played clarinet in my high school's concert band. Right after graduation, I got a job at Disney. I played in the orchestra at the Grand Floridian Hotel—it paid pretty decently—and that was my job for the past year."

"What'll you do for work in San Jose?"

Terrence rocked his head from side to side. "I have an audition scheduled with the Symphony Silicon Valley. And if that doesn't pan out, I'll find something else. Somebody always needs a clarinetist no matter where you go."

They crossed over US Highway 19, moving in a northwesterly direction. The region was dotted with lakes big and small, many surrounded by towering cypress trees festooned with Spanish moss. The lakes shimmered in the late-morning sun and Levi slipped on his sunglasses, a stylish pair with reflective polarized lenses.

Again, they kept quiet for a while. The only sounds in the van were air rushing through the windows and the engine's hum.

When Levi reached to turn on the van's radio, Terrence told him, "Don't bother; it doesn't work."

Levi clenched his teeth and silently cursed. No music for nearly three thousand miles? For the tenth time since he'd arrived at Terrence's house, he asked himself if he'd made a mistake by agreeing to drive the van to the West Coast. The van was no Crown Victoria—that was for certain—but on the other hand, it *did* seem to run smoothly. And though Terrence was a little odd, at least he wasn't a chatterbox. He seemed content to ride in silence with his gaze fixed on the windshield.

Near the small town of Wildwood, they paid their toll, each boy contributing half. Terrence kept his money in a zippered pouch with a bank's logo on it. Using a pencil, he noted the cost of half the toll on a spiral notepad he kept in the pouch. Then he returned the pouch to a box located behind the driver's seat.

They left the turnpike and then drove northward on I-75, a six-lane highway bisected by a grassy median. They passed billboards for retirement communities that offered idyllic lifestyles filled with golf, tennis, and swimming pools. Levi noticed the women on the billboards always looked twenty years younger than their husbands.

Once they'd passed Gainesville, they encountered dense slash pine forests. They passed cattle ranches and the occasional pecan grove. Billboards at several exits advertised tourist traps where taxidermic gator heads and saltwater taffy were sold. By the time they reached Lake City, where I-75 intersected with I-10, the time was close to noon and Levi's stomach was growling.

"I'm hungry," he told Terrence. "Why don't we stop for lunch?"

They chose a rest area shaded by live oaks and long leaf pines. The place had picnic tables, restrooms, and vending machines. From a box in the van, Terrence retrieved a peanut butter and jelly sandwich and a bottle of spring water. Levi opened his ice cooler. He slathered two pieces of white bread with mayo and mustard, and then he built himself a ham and cheese sandwich. He yanked a can of cola from the cooler, and then the two boys dined at a concrete picnic table while traffic roared past them on the interstate.

Levi spoke between bites from his sandwich. "At some point—maybe when we reach Pensacola—we can hit a supermarket to buy food for dinner and breakfast. Tonight I can sauté chicken strips with veggies and serve it over pasta. Then I'll cook bacon and eggs for breakfast tomorrow morning."

Terrence shook his head. "I can't eat a lot of what you just mentioned; I'm an ovo-lacto vegetarian."

Levi made a face. "A what?"

"I don't eat meat, fish, or poultry."

"Why not?"

Terrence shrugged. "I don't think eating animals or fish is healthy for you. I've been a vegetarian for two years now, and I don't miss meat at all."

Levi shook his head. "What *do* you eat?"

Terrence ticked off categories on his fingers. "Vegetables; whole grain bread and pasta; all kinds of nuts; brown rice; cheese and milk; peanut butter and eggs."

Levi worked his jaw from side to side.

"Look," Terrence said, "you eat whatever you want, and then maybe you can show me how to fix the kind of stuff I like. I've got to learn how to cook sometime, so it might as well be now."

Levi shrugged.

A chunky gray-haired man in a pair of work pants and a matching shirt approached. He carried a stick with a nail protruding from its lower end, along with a plastic garbage bag, and as he neared the boys, he stabbed a chewing gum wrapper that lay on the pine-needle-strewn ground. Then he dropped the wrapper into his bag.

"Hey, fellas," he said. "Enjoying your lunch?"

Terrence and Levi nodded.

"This is a great place to take a break," the old guy said. "I've worked maintenance here for six months, and I never get tired of it. Sure beats sitting at home with the old lady, know what I mean?" The guy winked at Levi and swung his gaze to Terrence.

"What age are you, son?"

"Nineteen," Terrence said.

"Mind if I ask you a question?"

Terrence shrugged.

"Have you ever gone camping in the woods with a bunch of guys?"

A puzzled expression appeared on Terrence's face. "Sure. Why?"

The old guy shifted his weight from one leg to the other while he kept on. "Let me ask you something else. Let's say you were camping like that, and one morning, you woke up in your tent with a sore butthole and jelly stains in your underwear. Would you tell anyone?"

Terrence looked at Levi with his eyebrows knitted. Then he looked at the old guy and shook his head.

The old guy's gaze drilled into Terrence's. "Want to go camping?"

Terrence's jaw sagged while the old guy burst into laughter. The old guy shook his head and twirled the stick in his hand like a majorette. Then he walked away, still laughing, with his garbage sack swaying.

Terrence looked at Levi with one corner of his mouth turned down while he shook his head. "What was *that* all about?"

Levi shrugged. "He has a weird sense of humor, I guess."

"You don't think he was serious?"

Levi wasn't sure what to say, so he took the path of least resistance. "It was a joke. He's just bored and looking to have some fun."

Terrence gazed at the tabletop and scowled.

Chapter Three

CHICKASABOGUE STATE PARK bordered Chickasaw Creek, just a short distance from I-65 and only a half-hour's drive northwest of Mobile. Levi and Terrence paid their camping fee at the park's office, and then they drove to their campsite, a pretty area shaded by slash pines. The site had a picnic table and a fire pit, and they even had a view of the creek. The creek water was greenish in color, and the banks were studded with bald cypress trees. Few people were using the park, probably because the day was Thursday, Levi figured. Tomorrow night, he told himself, the campground would likely be full of families.

After Levi pitched his dome-shaped tent and rolled out his sleeping bag, the boys hiked a trail that wound through a hardwood forest; they crushed oak leaves beneath their shoes. The sun was low in the sky, and they walked in shadows.

"So," Levi asked Terrence, "how come your license got suspended?"

"Too many speeding tickets. I kept running late for work at Disney. Whenever it happened, I'd do ninety on I-4 and get pulled over. After a half-dozen times, the DMV yanked it."

"How soon do you get your license back?"

Terrence grimaced. "About three months. I haven't been able to drive since May."

"That's got to be rough," Levi said.

Terrence nodded. "I feel like I'm fifteen again. If I need to go somewhere, I have to ask one of my grandparents for a ride. And a lot of the time they're not around, so then I have to walk."

A loud knocking sound came from above them. They looked up at a southern pileated woodpecker with white stripes on its flanks and a crimson crest on its head. The bird chipped away at a live oak's bark, and the sound of the knocking echoed through the forest.

"I never saw one so big," Terrence said.

"The kind we have in Florida are a different type of bird," Levi said. "They're smaller."

They walked on.

Levi asked Terrence, "How come you live with your grandparents?"

Terrence shoved his hands into his pockets; he rubbed his lips together before he answered, and Levi guessed that the question was one often asked of Terrence.

"My parents divorced when I was eight. My dad moved to Pennsylvania right after that, and we don't stay in touch. My mom died from breast cancer four years ago, so my grandparents are the only family I have."

"No brothers or sisters?"

"Nope."

Levi tried to imagine himself in Terrence's position but couldn't. Levi's family had always been large and tight-knit. He had an older brother in dental school and a little sister who was junior class president at Merritt Island High. His parents' marriage was rock-solid. All four of his grandparents lived in Brevard County, as did many aunts, uncles, and cousins, so holidays at the McKane homestead were more like tribal gatherings.

Now the trail brought Levi and Terrence back to Chickasaw Creek, where they sat on a dock, watching a team of wood ducks paddle about in the fading sunlight. Already, crickets chirped in the surrounding trees.

Levi thought back to his visit with Terrence to a Pensacola supermarket hours before. Rather than buying food jointly, they decided to do it separately. Terrence bought a jar of roasted peanuts, a block of cheddar cheese, a jar of peanut butter, another of jelly, a loaf of whole wheat bread, a carton of eggs, another of butter, a half gallon of fat-free milk, and two cans of vegetable soup. Levi bought a chicken breast, a can of baked beans, another of new potatoes, a bottle of OJ, his own carton of eggs, and a half pound of bacon. After they'd stored the perishables in Levi's ice cooler and the rest in a cardboard box, Terrence recorded the cost of his purchases on his notepad.

Now, on the dock, Levi asked Terrence, "Are you getting hungry?"

Terrence nodded.

"Let's grab showers first," Levi said, "and then I'll get cooking."

The men's lavatory had separate shower stalls with changing nooks. Levi took one stall while Terrence used an adjacent one, and soon the room clouded with steam; it smelled of soap and shampoo.

Levi spoke loudly enough so Terrence could hear him over the sound of rushing water. "So, this isn't your first time camping?"

"Actually," Terrence said, "it is."

"But you told the guy at the rest stop you'd camped before."

"I only lied 'cause I didn't want him to think I was a wimp. I've never been in a campground or slept in a tent. This is all new to me."

While Levi cleaned his ears with a washcloth, he told Terrence, "My family always took camping vacations when I was growing up. We pitched tents everywhere from the Florida Keys to the Smoky Mountains."

"I've never even *seen* a mountain," Terrence said. "What's it like to be so high up?"

Levi turned off his shower. Then he toweled himself. "It's amazing," he said. "In western North Carolina there's no air pollution; you can see for miles."

Moments later, they stood side by side at the sinks, combing their damp hair while gazing into a wall mirror. Both were shirtless, and for the first time, Levi saw just how slender Terrence was. Levi could count every rib in Terrence's torso. Could he possibly weigh more than one hundred and thirty pounds?

Back at their campsite, Levi lit his propane lantern. Then he set up his cook stove on their picnic table. Terrence sat on one of the table's benches, watching. After Levi opened two cans of beer, he handed one to Terrence, who looked at the can like it was something ominous.

"Something wrong?" Levi said.

Terrence nodded. "I've never drank alcohol before."

"You're kidding?"

Terrence shook his head. "I'm not twenty-one, so how would I buy it?"

Levi slurped from his own can. Then he told Terrence, "I get mine with a fake ID, one I bought on the Internet. Go on, give the beer a try; it'll relax you."

Terrence sipped from his can. Then he made a face like he'd swallowed medicine. "It has a bitter taste; I don't think I like it."

"Finish the can," Levi said. "You'll get used to the taste *real* quickly if you do."

Levi set about sautéing his chicken breast in a pan coated with olive oil. He got his beans and potatoes simmering in a saucepan on the stove's second burner. Then he told Terrence, "I'll warm up your soup right after my chicken is done. Sound good?"

Terrence nodded. Then, after he burped, he said, "If I get drunk, don't let me do something stupid, okay?"

Levi looked at Terrence and shook his head. "You won't get buzzed off one beer. I promise you that."

A few minutes passed while Terrence sipped from his beer. Then he asked Levi, "Do you feel like hearing some music?"

Levi crinkled his forehead. "What kind?"

"Clarinet; I told you I play."

Levi shrugged.

Terrence ambled to the van. Then he returned to the picnic table with the black plastic case Levi had seen when he'd loaded his things into the van back in Orlando. Terrence sat at the table; he opened the hasps on the case. Its interior was lined in blue velour. Pieces of the clarinet rested inside impressions that were sized to fit them, and Terrence set about assembling the instrument while Levi watched.

"How long have you played?" Levi asked.

Terrence answered while he fit together the clarinet's two longest pieces, the parts with the metal keypads on them. "I started when I was in third grade. My grandpa plays, and he got me interested. I joined the concert band when I got to middle school; I've played ever since."

After the clarinet was fully assembled, Terrence stuck the mouthpiece between his lips. Then he dampened the reed with his tongue while bobbing his head. He played a few scales as a warm-up, and the sounds the clarinet produced seemed both spooky and seductive to Levi.

Terrence told Levi, "I'm going to play 'My Heart Will Go On' from the movie *Titanic*. Ever heard it?"

Levi rocked his head from side to side while he stirred his beans and potatoes. "I mean, I saw the movie on TV once, but I don't remember any of the music."

Terrence played the song and Levi liked it very much. The clarinet produced a rich tone, and the tune itself had a lilt that Levi enjoyed. The song lasted about three minutes, and when Terrence finished it, Levi put down his spoon and clapped while Terrence blushed.

"Play something else," Levi said.

Terrence reached for his beer, took a healthy gulp from it, and then looked at Levi. "This next song is called 'A Whole New World'; it's from the movie *Aladdin*. Seen it?"

Levi shook his head and then Terrence played. The pitch of the notes rose and fell, and the sounds produced by the clarinet echoed off surrounding trees. Terrence played with his eyes closed, and Levi wondered what sort of thoughts dwelled in Terrence's head while he performed.

After Terrence finished "A Whole New World," he played two other songs: "The Pink Panther" by Henry Mancini and "Hedwig's Theme" from the Harry Potter movies.

Then Levi told Terrence, "My food's done. Why don't you get your soup and I'll put it on a burner to heat up."

Terrence nodded. After he disassembled his clarinet, he put the parts in the case. He returned the case to the van and brought one can of vegetable soup to the table, along with his block of cheddar cheese, a jar of peanuts, and milk jug. He ate handfuls of peanuts while he watched Levi empty the can's contents into a saucepan.

"So you never cook at home?" Levi asked.

Terrence shook his head. "My grandma does it. I just eat."

"Heating soup's about as easy as it gets," Levi said when he placed the saucepan on a burner. "You want to cook it on low heat and keep stirring so it warms up evenly. Understand?"

Terrence nodded.

"So," Levi said, "who will cook when you move in with your friend?"

Terrence lowered his gaze and shrugged. "We haven't talked about that yet."

Levi crinkled his forehead. "Exactly what *do* you guys talk about?"

Terrence shrugged again, but he didn't answer Levi's question. Instead, he gazed at something over Levi's shoulder.

Chapter Four

THE NEXT MORNING, songbirds chirped in the forest and a rising sun crested treetops to the east while Levi spoke to Terrence like a schoolteacher might.

"After you break the eggs into a bowl, you add a few drops of milk to them. Then you beat them with a fork to get a little air inside them; that makes them fluff up."

The boys sat at their picnic table while Levi demonstrated with four eggs. Then he dumped the eggs into a frying pan that perched over one burner on the cook stove. On the other burner, a coffeepot perked, and the aroma of brewing coffee wafted through the air. Three strips of freshly fried bacon rested on a paper towel.

Terrence's hair looked like he'd just left a wind tunnel. His eyes were swollen. He yawned twice, and then he rubbed the side of his face with the palm of his hand. "I didn't sleep too well," he told Levi. "The van's floor is hard and bumpy, and my sleeping bag doesn't have much padding."

Levi stirred the eggs with a spatula. "My tent's a two-man. We can share it if you'd like. The ground's softer than a metal floor."

Terrence raised his dark eyebrows. "You wouldn't mind?"

"It's no big deal," Levi said. "There's plenty of room."

Terrence spread butter over a slice of whole wheat bread. Then the boys ate their eggs off paper plates. Terrence guzzled OJ straight from the jug.

Levi chewed on a bacon strip. After he'd swallowed, he told Terrence, "Houston's about five hundred miles from here. We can stay at Stephen Austin State Park, west of the city. I'll call and reserve a campsite before we leave here this morning. Sound good?"

Terrence nodded.

Once they'd finished eating, Levi poured mugs of coffee for himself and Terrence. Terrence dumped three spoonfuls of sugar into his mug before he sipped from it tentatively. "I don't normally drink coffee," he said. "I'm nervous enough without adding caffeine to the mix."

"What are you so nervous about?"

Terrence shifted his weight on his bench while he answered. "Everything, I guess. I was always an outsider in school, never one of the cool kids. I suck at sports, and even though I'm nineteen, most people think I'm much younger. Do you know what all that feels like?"

Levi shook his head.

Terrence said, "It makes me uncomfortable around people because I know they look down on me. They think I'm a geek, like that maintenance guy at the rest stop yesterday. Do you think he'd say that sort of thing to you?"

Levi didn't respond. What was there to say?

Once they'd finished their coffee, Terrence loaded up the dirty frying pan, coffeepot, and other items into a plastic dish tub. He took these and a bottle of dish soap to the men's lavatory where he washed them in an outdoor sink the campground provided. By the time Terrence was finished, Levi had already folded up his tent and placed it in the van along with their other belongings. They brushed their teeth, using a jug of drinking water, and then it was time to leave.

"I kind of like this place," Terrence said to Levi as they drove toward the park's exit. "You chose a good spot."

Levi shrugged. "I've stayed in better, but also in a lot worse. I think we did okay."

Once back on I-10, they quickly reached the Alabama-Mississippi state line. Pines and oaks lined the road shoulders, but just beyond the trees were corn and cotton fields. They even passed a watermelon field where workers in broad-brimmed straw hats gathered fruit from the vines and loaded them into the bed of a pickup truck. The sky was overcast, which Levi considered a blessing since it kept the temperature down a good deal, and he wondered if perhaps they'd encounter rain during the day.

They stopped in Biloxi to fill their gas tank, and while Terrence cleaned the windshield with a squeegee, Levi checked the oil level in the van's engine. Each of them paid for half the gas in cash, and like always, Terrence wrote down the amount he'd spent in his spiral notepad.

The Bo Peep van hummed. They passed by Biloxi and then Gulfport before entering Louisiana. They were close enough to the Gulf of Mexico that Levi could smell saltwater in the air that rushed through the cab. The briny scent reminded him of Brevard County.

"Ever been to New Orleans?" Terrence asked Levi.

Levi said no.

"I've always wanted to spend time in the French Quarter, so I could listen to jazz music there. The clarinet's huge in jazz, you know—every band has at least one—and a lot of songs have clarinet solos in them. Ever heard of Alvin Batiste?" Terrence said.

"Who?"

"Alvin Batiste; he was a jazz clarinetist from New Orleans. He's not alive now, but he was a giant in his time. He's one of my heroes."

Levi tried to concentrate on what Terrence was saying, but his thoughts kept returning to his conversation with Taylor at Taco City. She'd given no indication that her mind might change about terminating her pregnancy, and that had Levi worriedBy noon, they had passed Lake Pontchartrain. They found a wayside park in a town called Livingston where they dined on sandwiches under shade cast by live oaks draped in Spanish moss. Off in the distance, an oil rig creaked and groaned. Terrence drank from his milk jug in between bites from his cheese sandwich.

"You seem awfully quiet today," he told Levi. "Did I say something wrong?"

Levi shook his head. "I'm not a talkative person by nature; plus right now I have a lot on my mind."

"Like what?"

Levi pondered how much he should tell Terrence about the situation with Taylor. Then he told himself, *hell, once we reach San Jose, I'll never see this guy again.*

"I met a girl this summer," he said. Then he told the whole story in detail while Terrence listened intently. The words *spilled* out of Levi like water from an open spigot—he probably said more in ten minutes than he normally said in a month—and he actually felt relieved when he concluded his narrative.

"Are you sure the baby is yours?" Terrence asked.

Levi grimaced. "Pretty sure. We probably had sex a half-dozen times this summer, and as far as I know, she wasn't seeing anyone else."

"What'll you do about it?"

"That's what I've been asking myself all morning," Levi said. "I want her to get an abortion, but she's not keen on it. If she decides not to, I might have a problem on my hands."

Terrence took another bite from his sandwich. After he swallowed, he said, "It doesn't seem fair, does it? Why should the decision only be hers to make?"

Levi nodded; then Terrence asked, "Do her parents know?"

Levi drew a breath and let it out. "Not yet, but they will soon enough if she doesn't have the abortion, and they won't be happy about it either."

"Wow," Terrence said while shaking his head, "and I thought *I* had problems."

"What problems?" Levi asked.

Terrence shifted his weight on the picnic bench while he moistened his lips. "My grandparents aren't in good health. They're selling their house *and* the Bo Peep business. Then they'll move into assisted living. It's all supposed to happen within the next six weeks, and when it does, I'm homeless."

"So get an apartment."

Terrence shook his head.

"Why not?" Levi asked.

"I can't live alone; I wouldn't know how to. I can't cook or do laundry or anything else when it comes to housekeeping, plus falling asleep in an empty apartment sounds kind of...creepy."

Levi shrugged. "Share a place with a friend in Orlando."

Terrence shook his head again. "I don't have any friends, not anymore. I had a few in high school, but after we graduated, they didn't stay in touch. And the folks I work with at Disney are all much older than me; we don't have anything in common other than the music we play."

"So that's why you're moving to California, so you won't have to live alone?"

"It's a big part of it," Terrence said.

"And what's the rest?"

Terrence opened his mouth to speak, but then an eighteen-wheeler pulled into the park; it halted just a short distance from where Levi and Terrence sat. The driver left his diesel engine running while he exited the truck and headed for the park's restrooms. The diesel's rattling sound made it impossible for Levi and Terrence to talk in a normal fashion, and the fumes emanating from the truck's chrome exhaust pipe made both boys crinkle their noses.

Levi rose and began to gather his things. "Come on," he hollered at Terrence. "Let's clear out of this place before my eardrums burst."

An hour after they'd eaten lunch, Levi and Terrence crossed the Mississippi River at Baton Rouge, a city of nondescript architecture, save for the state capitol building, an art deco structure that towered over most everything else in town. The bridge crossing the river looked to Levi like something he might've built with his erector set when he was a kid, and the water flowing beneath them was browned by the silt it carried.

"*That's* the Mississippi River?" Terrence said.

"That's it."

Terrence shook his head while he stared out the passenger window. "How ugly, and I'll bet it's so dirty you can't even swim in it."

Levi recalled thinking similar thoughts when he'd first crossed the river on this same bridge back in May and he had tried to imagine Huckleberry Finn and Jim floating on their raft in the muddy water but couldn't. Was the river cleaner back then?

Terrence reached for his clarinet case. He assembled the pieces and wetted his reed. Then he told Levi, "I'm going to play 'Down to Memphis' by JJ Cale, ever heard it?"

Levi shook his head.

Terrence shrugged. "It's the only song I know that talks about the Mississippi."

The Cale tune had a chirpy quality to it that Levi enjoyed, and he liked the way the notes Terrence played sort of floated through the van's interior. He found himself tapping his fingers on the steering wheel to the song's rhythm, and when the song ended, he was smiling.

"You're pretty good with that thing," he told Terrence.

Terrence looked at Levi and smiled while his cheeks reddened. Then he said, "As long as I've got my clarinet out, why don't I play an Alvin Batiste song?"

"Do it," Levi said.

"This one's called 'Words of Wisdom,'" Terrence said and then he played the tune. Unlike the Cale number, the Batiste song had a wistful sound and a quirky beat, but Levi liked it anyway. The notes rose and fell as they drove through farm country and forest, all of it lush and green. Levi watched Terrence's delicate fingers work the keypads on the clarinet, and for the first time, Levi noticed how Terrence's fingernails were bitten to their quicks.

When Terrence finished the Batiste number, he disassembled the clarinet and returned the pieces to their proper places in the case. Then he snapped the case shut and stowed it behind him. Thereafter, neither of them spoke for about an hour. They passed through a cypress swamp with huge trees rising from dark and placid water. Levi spotted a white egret wading, a splash of brightness in all that darkness. Then he thought about Taylor again. Back at Taco City, he had promised he would call her this evening—and he still planned to—but he had no idea what he would say to her. The more he thought about their last conversation, the more discouraged he felt. Based on Taylor's body language at Taco City, he could pretty much tell an abortion wasn't going to happen, and assuming that was the case, what were his options?

If he refused to marry Taylor—and he planned on doing exactly that—maybe Taylor would put the baby up for adoption. Wouldn't that excuse Levi from any obligation to the child? And maybe, just maybe, a paternity test would prove the child wasn't his. But he was pretty sure it *was* his child, and if Taylor kept the baby, what next?

Terrence's cell phone chimed. He yanked it from his pocket, pushed the Talk button and said hello. Then a conversation ensued, one Levi heard only one side of.

"We're in Louisiana; we just crossed the Mississippi River."

"No, I'm not sure; maybe Tuesday."

Terrence glanced at Levi. "Yeah, he's fine," he said. A few seconds passed, then he said, "Me too; I'll talk to you later."

Terrence put his phone back in his pocket; he drummed his fingers on the sill of the passenger door.

"Was that your friend in San Jose?" Levi asked.

Terrence nodded.

Levi kneaded the steering wheel. "So, where on the Internet did you two meet?"

Terrence looked at Levi for a second or two before returning his gaze to the windshield. "I don't remember the name of the site."

"How old is this guy?"

"Thirty-five; his name is Hsueh-Yu. He's Taiwanese—an engineer at a tech company."

Levi made a face. The whole situation seemed fishy, like Terrence wasn't fully explaining things. "I don't get it," Levi said. "Exactly what's going on between you and your friend?"

Terrence's temples grew pink. He swung his gaze to Levi and narrowed his eyes. "We're going to live together as a couple in San Jose. Do you have a problem with that?"

Levi returned his gaze to the highway while he licked his lips. "No problem at all—honestly—but you've never met this guy in person, so how do you know...."

"What?"

"That you'll get along with each other? Chatting online is one thing, but living together is another. What if things don't work out? Then you've driven three thousand miles for nothing."

Terrence crossed his arms over his chest. He stared out the windshield with a scowl on his face.

"I'll *make* it work out. I don't really have a choice, now do I?"

Chapter Five

CONVERSATION LESSENED TO a trickle after the discussion about Terrence's San Jose friend. Levi didn't want to seem pushy by asking more questions, and Terrence didn't seem inclined to discuss his plans in more detail. They passed by the town of Lafayette and then Lake Charles, where a gambling casino seemed to be the biggest thing going on. Then they entered Texas, which to Levi looked pretty much like western Louisiana. The first Texas city they encountered was Beaumont, a sizeable river town where they shopped for food at an H-E-B supermarket and then moved on to Houston, where Terrence gushed over the skyscrapers they passed.

"I've never seen such tall buildings," he said while shaking his head. "I didn't know they could make them so high."

The Stephen F. Austin State Park wasn't much of a park. It fronted the Brazos River. The camping area was nothing more than an oak grove where the underbrush had been cleared and replaced with crabgrass. But the camping fee wasn't much and their campsite had a picnic table and a fire pit with a heavy iron grill. About 50 percent of the campsites were occupied, mostly by families with small children or retirees in RVs.

The time was fast approaching 6:00 p.m., and Levi busied himself by pitching his tent on a patch of grass. He knelt on the ground and was pounding on a tent stake with a rock when Terrence approached and cleared his throat.

He said to Levi, "Can I ask you a question?"

Levi looked up.

Terrence drew a breath and let it out while he ran a hand through his hair. "Are you still okay with me sharing your tent?"

"Sure," Levi said. "Why wouldn't I be?"

Terrence shifted his weight from one leg to the other while he talked. "Now that you know I'm gay, I thought you might be uncomfortable sleeping next to me."

"It's fine," Levi said.

"You're sure?"

Levi nodded. "Go get your sleeping bag and pillow."

Back at Merritt Island High, there had been no openly gay students when Levi attended. And in conservative Brevard County, whatever gay population existed kept to itself. But at Stanford, being gay was sort of like having red hair. No one cared if two boys walked through campus holding hands.

When Terrence returned to the tent with his bag and pillow, Levi unrolled the bag next to his own, inside the tent, and then he placed Terrence's pillow atop the pink bag. A space of two feet separated the bags.

"I really appreciate this," Terrence said while he watched what Levi was doing. "Sleeping in that van was super crappy."

Levi nodded while he rose and dusted off his knees. "Let's grab showers. Then I'll get busy on dinner."

While they strolled toward the shower house with towels slung over their shoulders, Levi pondered his conversation with Terrence back near the Mississippi. "Look," he said to Terrence now, "I hope I didn't embarrass you when I asked about your friend in San Jose."

"It's okay," Terrence said while he fiddled with the zipper on his toiletry bag. "It's just that I'm not used to talking about the situation."

"Your grandparents don't know?"

Terrence shook his head. "Nobody does but you."

Inside the shower house, there were two shower stalls, but no private place to undress was offered, just a bench with clothing hooks on the wall above it. Levi placed his shaving kit and his change of clothes on the bench and pulled his T-shirt over his head. He hung the shirt on a hook while Terrence stood as still as a statue, watching Levi and flexing his fingers at his hips.

When Levi noticed Terrence's inactivity, he crinkled his forehead.

"Is something wrong?"

Terrence's face reddened, and then his voice broke like a bar mitzvah boy's when he answered.

"I'm not used to undressing in front of other people. It feels...uncomfortable."

Levi shrugged. Then he popped the button at his waist and dropped his shorts to his ankles. He stepped out of the shorts and hung them on a hook. Then he followed suit with his boxer shorts while Terrence sat on the bench and unlaced a sneaker. He wouldn't look at Levi; he kept his gaze low and waited until Levi was inside a shower stall before he undressed.

Within moments, the air steamed, and Levi had to raise his voice to be heard above the sound of rushing water. "I need to phone Taylor tonight; I promised her I would."

"What'll you say to her?" Terrence asked.

"That's just it," Levi said. "I don't know."

"I guess you've met her folks?"

"Oh, yeah. I had dinner at their house one night. Her dad's an overbearing military type who thinks he's king of the hill, and her mom's at morning mass every day of the week."

Levi smelled the coconut-scented shampoo Terrence used.

"My grandparents are Catholic," Terrence said. "My grandpa doesn't always attend church, but Grandma's there each Sunday and she says her prayers at night."

Levi recalled the bathtub Madonna at Terrence's house. "What about you? Are you religious?"

"Not at all. My mom didn't try to force it on me, and I never had an interest in going to church. I'd rather sleep in on Sunday mornings."

A few minutes passed without conversation. When Terrence emerged from his stall, he already wore his fresh briefs. Levi was still naked and toweled himself at the bench. He honestly didn't care whether Terrence looked at him or not, but Terrence went out of his way *not* to look at Levi. He kept his gaze low until Levi had partially dressed himself, and only then did he stare at Levi with his nose crinkled when he spoke.

"I can't believe how casual you are about getting naked in front of me."

Levi shrugged. "It's not a big deal. I know you're not going to grab me."

Terrence drew back and made a face. "What makes you think I'd do that?"

Levi looked at Terrence. Then he placed his index finger on his chest. "Do you think I'm good looking? Be honest." Levi had never spent time with a gay boy before—not that he knew of anyway—and he was curious if Terrence felt an attraction to him.

"You're a handsome guy," Terrence said while he pulled a fresh T-shirt over his head. Then he looked at Levi again. "But I shouldn't think of you in a sexual way, not if we're going to share your tent."

When they returned to their campsite, Levi excused himself. He walked out of earshot, punched up Taylor's number on his phone. She answered on the third ring, sounding breathless.

"Why are you panting?" Levi asked.

"I was in the backyard and my phone was in the house. I had to run before your call went to voice mail. So, where are you?"

Levi explained. Then he said, "Can you talk?"

"Sure," Taylor said. "Just let me go to my room so no one overhears."

Seconds later, a click sounded as a door closed. Then Taylor said, "Have you given any more thought to our situation? Now that I'm a baby momma, I don't like all this uncertainty."

Levi cringed at hearing those two words—baby momma. It seemed to him that Taylor was actually *proud* of her pregnancy like it somehow validated her existence. "Look, I'm not ready for fatherhood. I have two years of college to go, and I may attend grad school after that."

"You don't want to be part of your child's upbringing?"

Levi felt like screaming. He ran his fingers through his hair while he stared into the limbs of a nearby live oak. Then he did his best to speak in an even tone. "If the circumstances were different, of course, I would. But I'll be in California and you'll be in Florida—it just won't work. Abortion is the best choice for both of us and probably for the baby too. Single-parent homes aren't good for kids."

Taylor was silent for a few seconds. Then she told Levi, "I saw a lawyer this morning. She says if you're the father, then you'll have to pay child support until the baby turns eighteen."

Shit.

Levi paced at an empty campsite. He glanced here and there. "I don't have *money* to pay child support; I'm a student."

"Then maybe your parents will pay it for you."

"They won't; I guarantee you that."

"You could be held in contempt of court and sent to jail if you didn't pay each week; that's what the lawyer told me today. I'd hate to see it happen, but...."

Levi raised his voice a couple of notches. "Just get the abortion, will you? It solves all our problems and neither your parents nor mine will ever know."

A few moments of silence passed while Levi held his breath.

"You're sure you won't marry me?"

Levi exhaled. "Positive. It's not going to happen."

"I could make you happy if you'd only let me."

"No, you couldn't," Levi said.

BACK AT THE campsite, Levi found Terrence seated at their picnic table and talking on his cell phone. Terrence's unopened clarinet case rested on the bench he sat on.

"Grandma, it's going fine, so stop worrying about me. Tonight I'll sleep in Levi's tent 'cause the van's not really comfortable."

Levi set up his propane stove on the picnic table while Terrence continued to talk.

"Yeah," Terrence said, glancing at Levi, "we're getting along great. Tomorrow we'll drive to west Texas; I'll give you a call from there around dinnertime. Sound good?"

When Terrence concluded his phone call, Levi broke out two beers. He handed one to Terrence and opened the other for himself. Levi started cooking his meal on his stove while Terrence played a few tunes on his clarinet: the theme from *Star Wars*, then "New York, New York," and then "Stairway to Heaven," which Levi especially liked. After he clapped his approval, he brought out two more beers.

Terrence drained whatever was left of his first beer and opened a second. Already his posture had relaxed. He sat on the picnic table's bench, watching Levi boil noodles for macaroni and cheese.

"How are your grandparents doing?" Levi asked Terrence. "Do they miss you?"

Terrence nodded. "They don't understand why I'm doing this. If they had their way, I'd stay in Orlando so I could visit them at the ALF, but I just can't. It's my goal to share life with another man—someone I really care for—and they wouldn't approve."

Levi nodded but still couldn't understand Terrence's plan.

"Mind if I ask you something personal?"

Terrence raised his eyebrows. "What's that?"

"Have you ever *had* a boyfriend?"

Terrence lowered his gaze and shook his head.

"Then how do you know you're gay?"

Terrence shifted his weight on the bench. "Believe me, I know."

Levi opened a can of green beans using a manual can opener. Then he emptied the beans into a second pot that he placed on the stove. After he lit a burner, he set it on low. Then he looked at Terrence again. "Can I ask you another personal question?"

"Go ahead."

"Have you experienced sex with a guy?"

Terrence's cheeks colored while he stared at the tabletop and bobbed his chin. "Only once." He looked up at Levi. "A man in the orchestra at Disney got together with me. He's about forty and married but sees guys on the side. I guess you'd say he's bisexual."

"How was it?"

Terrence shrugged. "Not as good as I'd hoped. Plus I was sore for like...two days afterward."

Levi winced. "What's this man in San Jose like?"

After Terrence sipped from his beer, he smacked his lips. "He's tall and thin and he's handsome, at least *I* think so. Like all Chinese guys, he has dark hair and eyes. And he's a top."

"A top?"

Terrence nodded. "He'll pitch and I'll catch. But first I have to learn to relax down there. Understand?"

Levi made a face. "I'm not sure I could *ever* do that."

"You're straight, so you don't have to."

"Tell me one more thing," Levi said while he stirred the beans. "If you could choose to be heterosexual, would you?"

Terrence puckered one side of his face while he shifted his weight on the picnic bench. He rubbed the tip of his nose with a knuckle. "It's kind of a useless question, isn't it? I *can't* choose, so why even wonder what I'd do if I could? I like men; that's just me, and it's not going to change. So I need to find a guy I'll be happy with."

Levi poured cooking oil into a frying pan. He took the pot of steaming beans off one burner and commenced frying a pork chop. The chop hissed and popped over the burner.

"So, do you think this San Jose guy will be the right one for you?"

Terrence sipped his beer again before he answered. "Once I heard his voice, I was pretty sure we'd be a good match. It's a deep voice. And when he talks, it's like I'm listening to a musical instrument, the way it goes up and down."

Levi didn't say anything because he wasn't sure he understood Terrence's response.

"We're always talking about me," Terrence said. "What about you? When did you first have sex?"

Levi prodded the pork chop with a spatula. "I was fourteen. I did it with a neighbor girl in the back seat of her parents' car."

"You were *fourteen*?"

Levi nodded. "She was older than me, and the whole thing was her idea. It wasn't all that great and didn't last too long."

Terrence giggled.

"What is it?" Levi said.

"Nothing, just...."

"What?"

"No one has ever talked to me about stuff like this before."

After Levi flipped his pork chop, he gestured toward Terrence with the spatula. "Why don't you get your soup from the van? This chop will be done in just a few minutes, and then I can put the soup on."

Terrence nodded. While he ambled toward the van, Levi studied Terrence's slender frame. Back at Merritt Island High, Levi knew a guy like Terrence would have been a social outcast. But after spending two days with Terrence, Levi had warmed to him a good deal. Sure, he was somewhat naïve and a bit girlish, but Levi figured he could have done a lot worse when choosing a travel companion. At least Terrence wasn't obnoxious or lazy, and he was surprisingly easy to talk with.

By the time they ate their dinner and Terrence cleaned up, darkness had fallen and Levi was yawning. "It's been a long day," he told Terrence. "I'm ready to turn in."

Terrence said, "Me too," and Levi extinguished his propane lantern. He used a flashlight to illuminate his tent flaps while he unzipped them. Then he moved aside so Terrence could enter first. Levi followed and re-zipped the flaps so insects wouldn't get inside the tent. Levi wriggled out of all his clothes except his boxers, and Terrence did the same; he wore only his briefs when he climbed inside his sleeping bag. His head rested on his pillow.

The night was warm, and Levi lay atop his bag, staring up at the tent ceiling with his fingers interlaced behind his neck. He listened to Terrence breathe. "Comfortable?" he asked.

"Yeah, this is much better than the van. You're sure you're okay with me sleeping next to you?"

"Positive," Levi answered. "I'll see you in the morning."

LEVI WOKE TO the sound of whimpering. His eyelids fluttered open, and he realized the night was far from over.

The whimpering came from Terrence. He stirred inside his sleeping bag, making rustling sounds like he was rubbing his knees together. "Where are you?" he said in a shaky voice. "Why aren't you here?"

Levi flicked on his flashlight. Terrence lay on his side, facing away from Levi. Again he moved his knees, almost as if he were climbing a flight of stairs.

Levi reached for Terrence's shoulder and shook it lightly. "Hey, are you okay?"

A few seconds passed before Terrence flipped onto his back. He squinted at the brightness of the flashlight's beam. Then he asked Levi, "What is it?"

"You were talking in your sleep and making weird sounds, maybe having a bad dream."

Terrence scratched his head; his voice sounded reedy when he spoke. "What did I say?"

"It sounded like you were looking for someone you couldn't find."

"Did I say a name?"

Levi shook his head. Then he asked, "Are you feeling all right?"

"I think so," Terrence said. "But now I need to pee."

"Don't bother walking all the way to the bathhouse," Levi said. "Just take the flashlight and find yourself a tree. No one will see you."

Terrence didn't get dressed; he only slipped into his sneakers. A minute later, Terrence's stream gushed not all that far from the tent, and then Terrence returned, looking awkward in his briefs and sneakers as he crawled back through the tent flaps. His hair stood on end and his eyes looked puffy. After he kicked off his shoes, he got inside his sleeping bag. Then he handed the flashlight back to Levi.

Levi extinguished the flashlight. He told Terrence, "I checked my phone while you were gone. It's around three in the morning."

"And now I'm not sleepy," Terrence said.

"Maybe I shouldn't have woke you up, but you sounded distressed."

"Did I? I wonder what was going on inside my head."

"Couldn't tell you," Levi said while he rearranged his limbs, "but it didn't sound pleasant. Do you have bad dreams often?"

Terrence cleared his throat. "How would I know? At home, I have my own bedroom and I sleep with the door shut, so I don't think anyone would hear me making noises. And I never remember my dreams the next day. Anyway, I'm sorry I disturbed you."

"It's okay," Levi said. "But why don't we try to get some more sleep? We have a long drive to make tomorrow."

"Where is it we're going?"

"A town called Fort Stockton; it's a five-hundred-mile drive through some of the most boring countrysides you'll ever see."

"Where will we stay?"

"In an RV park. It's nothing special, but it'll do."

They lay in silence for a minute or so, and then Terrence spoke.

"Levi?"

"Hmmm?"

"Thanks for waking me up."

Chapter Six

A ROOSTER CROWING woke Levi from his slumber. The sun had just crested the eastern horizon when he peered out the tent's flaps. The morning air was cool and felt good on Levi's forehead. He turned to gaze at Terrence, who slept on his back. Levi studied Terrence's thick eyebrows, turned-up nose, and pink lips that reminded Levi of a flower. Terrence's milky skin was smooth and unblemished like porcelain.

"Time to get up," Levi said while he squeezed Terrence's shoulder. Then he watched as Terrence's long-lashed eyelids fluttered open.

"Let's hit the bathhouse," Levi said, "and then I'll get breakfast going."

Moments later, they stood side by side at a bank of urinals. While their streams made gurgling sounds, Levi stole a glance at Terrence's penis; it looked like a pale Vienna sausage with a *glans* that reminded Levi of a fat pencil eraser.

Back at the campsite, Levi fried bacon for himself. Both boys dined on eggs and toast at their picnic table and Terrence guzzled orange juice from his jug. Then they sipped from coffee mugs while Levi placed a call to the Ft. Stockton RV park to reserve a camping spot.

After the call, Levi told Terrence, "I hope you brought a bathing suit with you."

"Why?"

"The park has a swimming pool. It'll be a nice way to relax after our travel."

While Terrence cleaned up after breakfast, Levi rolled up both sleeping bags and removed them from the tent along with the pillows. Then he dismantled his tent. He stowed these things in the van. After they brushed their teeth at the bathhouse, they loaded Levi's cooking equipment, ice cooler, and propane lantern into the van, and then they left the park. Within twenty minutes, they had reached I-10, where they cruised at seventy miles per hour. Wind rushed into the van through the windows, but even the wind was warm, and Levi wasn't looking forward to the steamy drive ahead.

They rode in silence for a while. Terrence put his feet up on the dash and scratched his chest while he gazed out the windshield. The greenness of suburban west Houston quickly gave way to treeless prairie. They passed dozens of oil derricks that reminded Levi of birds drinking from mud puddles as their booms rose and fell. They passed a few cattle ranches, and then there was nothingness, just the stretch of road ahead of them, and never-ending sagebrush to either side.

"We should find some way to pass the time," Terrence said. "Maybe we could play a game of some kind."

"I can't play cards or checkers," Levi said. "I have to keep my gaze on the road and my hands on the wheel."

"How about Truth or Dare?" Terrence said.

Levi looked at Terrence and rolled his eyes. "I haven't played that since I was like...fifteen."

"Oh, come on," Terrence said. "It'll be fun."

Levi shrugged, "If you say so."

Terrence lowered his feet to the floor and turned to Levi. "You go first: choose truth or dare."

"Truth," Levi said.

Terrence lowered his gaze while he rubbed his index finger against his thumb. Then he looked at Levi and said, "What's the scariest thing that's ever happened to you?"

Levi stared out the windshield while he pondered the question. Then he told Terrence, "I was surfing at Sebastian Inlet when a spinner shark jumped out of the water. It knocked me off my board, and then a second shark bit me on my leg."

Terrence straightened his spine. "Holy crap. Did that really happen?"

Levi pointed to a V-shaped scar on his right calf. "I was so scared I crapped in my board shorts, no joke. Now it's your turn: truth or dare?"

Terrence rubbed his chin with a knuckle. "Truth."

"What the scariest thing that ever happened to *you?*" Levi asked.

Terrence shifted his weight in his seat. "That's an easy one; when I was eight, my mom took me to a carnival. You know—the kind with a Ferris wheel and all?"

Levi nodded.

"They had a spook house and I decided to go in. My mom paid the money and told me she'd wait outside. Well, I didn't know what I was getting into; there were all kinds of scary things in the house: monsters that jumped out at you from the darkness, spiderwebs that got in your face, you name it. And it was dark in there, very hard to see.

"Anyway, I wandered into this maze and I couldn't find my way out. All the time, these creepy sounds were going off around me—witches cackling and creatures moaning and women screaming. I started to think I wasn't ever going to get out of there, and then I started hollering for my mom to help me."

"So, what happened?" Levi asked.

"I guess the guy who ran the spook house finally heard me, or maybe someone else did and then they told him what was going on. He had to turn the lights on inside the house. Then he brought me outside to my mom. By then, I was crying and shaking so hard I could barely stand up."

Terrence shook his head. "I'll never forget it, actually. Even now, when I'm lying in bed at night, I'll think about that spook house and then I start trembling."

"You're kidding," Levi said.

"It's true," Terrence said. "Do you know the Haunted Mansion at Disney?"

Levi nodded.

"There's no *way* you'd get me to go in there," Terrence said. "Not even if you paid me a million dollars."

Terrence pointed at Levi. "Your turn. Truth or dare?"

Levi looked out the windshield again. Then he said, "Truth."

Terrence lowered his gaze and rubbed his lips together, then looked up at Levi with a little smile on his lips. "What's the most disgusting thing you've ever done?"

Levi knew the answer right away but wasn't sure that he should share the experience with Terrence. In fact, he'd never spoken of it to anyone.

Levi pointed a finger at Terrence's nose. "Don't ever tell anybody what I'm about to say, understand?"

Terrence nodded. "That's one of the rules of the game, right?"

Levi nodded. "When I was nine, this kid named Kevin was always picking on me and other kids at the school bus stop. He was two years older than me and a lot bigger. He'd call me a pussy and shove me around."

"How cruel."

"True, but I got my revenge."

"How?"

Levi snickered. "One morning before school, I crapped into an empty jelly jar. Then I put the lid on and brought the jar to the bus stop. While Kevin was bullying some other kid, he left his backpack untended. I emptied the turds into one of the pockets."

Terrence cackled and shook his head. "What a great story."

Levi shrugged. "Let's move on. It's your choice: truth or dare."

"Truth," Terrence said.

Levi asked Terrence a question he'd always wanted to ask another boy, but never had the nerve to. "Tell me the most times you've ever jerked off in a single day."

Terrence's cheeks turned crimson while he lowered his gaze.

"Come on," Levi said. "You know the answer; every guy does."

Terrence looked up and puffed out his cheeks. His gaze traveled from Levi to the highway and back. "Okay. When I was fifteen, one day I stayed home sick from school, only I wasn't really ill; I just didn't feel like going to classes. My grandparents and mom were working at Bo Peep, so I was alone. I had a gay porno magazine and jerked off to it...at least six times."

"Did you *come* every time?"

Terrence nodded, and then Levi whistled. "That's pretty impressive. I think *four* is my personal best; you must've been one horny kid."

"I still am," Terrence said. "You might not think so by looking at me, but sex is always on my mind; I don't know why. Even when I'm playing my clarinet, I'm thinking about some guy, you know...."

"What?"

"Fucking me."

Levi flinched at Terrence's reply because Terrence had never used crude language in Levi's presence before. But Levi shook it off. "What's that feel like?"

"Getting fucked?"

Levi nodded.

Terrence rocked his head from side to side. "It's okay. Like I told you, I've only done it once, with the guy from the orchestra. But I practice a lot and—"

"How do you *practice* getting fucked in the ass?"

"I'll show you." Terrence seized a cardboard box from behind the passenger seat, and after he parted the box's flaps, he produced a translucent latex dildo. Perhaps nine inches in length, the dildo wagged to and fro with the van's movement. Terrence looked up at Levi. "When I'm home alone, sometimes I'll lube this with jelly, and then I work it up inside me."

Levi made a face while he studied the dildo. "Doesn't it hurt?"

"Not if I take my time. It actually feels *good* once I relax."

Levi studied the road ahead of him while Terrence returned the dildo to the box and the box to its rightful place.

"Are we done playing Truth or Dare?" Terrence said when he settled back into the passenger seat.

"I guess we got sidetracked, didn't we?" Levi said. "Let's play some more. Whose turn is it to choose?"

"Yours."

Levi licked his lips. "We haven't done a dare yet. So I'll choose dare, but you have to choose dare on your next turn also. Agreed?"

"Okay." Terrence crossed his arms at his chest, then worked his jaw from side to side while he stared at Levi with narrowed eyes.

"What's your dare?" Levi said.

"I'm thinking about it. See you're kind of limited to what you can do when you're driving."

"True," Levi said. "You'll have to be creative."

Terrence nodded. He chewed a hangnail for a few seconds and then snapped his fingers. "I've got it." After he stuck an index finger up his nostril, he plucked out a greasy booger. "I dare you to let me put this on the tip of your nose. You'll have to leave it there for the rest of the day."

Levi looked at Terrence and hissed. "That is sick, man. Do you really expect me to do that?"

Terrence grinned and bobbed his chin.

Levi pointed a finger a Terrence. "I'm warning you—if you make me do this, you'll regret it when it's your turn."

"I'll take my chances," Terrence said.

Levi looked at the booger on the tip of Terrence's finger. He drew a breath and let it out. "Okay, go ahead."

After Terrence pasted the booger on the tip of Levi's nose, Levi saw it glistening there if he closed one eye.

Terrence guffawed while Levi shook his head.

"This is totally disgusting," Levi said. "I don't know why I let you do this to me."

"Oh, come on," Terrence said between laughs. "It's not hurting you, and no one else can see it but me. What's the big deal?"

Levi growled. "I'll ask you the same question in just a few minutes. Go ahead now, say *dare*."

"Dare."

Levi reached for the button on the waist of his khaki shorts. After he popped the button, he ran down his zipper. Then he wriggled out of the shorts completely.

"What are you doing?" Terrence said.

"You'll see," Levi replied.

Levi glanced in the van's rear and side-view mirrors to be sure no other motorists were around. Then he peeled off his boxer shorts while Terrence watched with his jaw sagged and his eyes bugged.

Levi handed the boxer shorts to Terrence. The boxers were white with a pattern of red hearts dancing across them, a Valentine's Day gift Levi's mom had sent him. "You're going to wear those on the top of your head for the rest of the day."

"What?"

"You heard me. I warned you, but you didn't listen, and now it's your turn to pay."

Terrence looked down at the boxers while he let out his breath. Then he lifted them to the crown of his head. He edged the elastic waistband downward until it reached the middle of his forehead and just above his ears. When he let go, the elastic gripped him like a headband. The bulk of the boxers hung from the crown of his head, almost reaching his shoulders, so he looked like he wore a woman's shower cap.

Levi roared while he stepped back into his khaki shorts and pulled them up his legs. "You look absolutely ridiculous. I'll have to take a picture to remember this by." Levi zipped up and buttoned his shorts. He looked at Terrence and said, "Are you happy now?"

Terrence crossed his arms at his chest and scowled. "It's not funny; you're humiliating me."

"No more than you did by sticking this crap on my nose," Levi said while he pointed at his face. Already the booger had lost its sheen as wind rushing through the van robbed it of moisture. The wind fluttered Levi's boxer shorts too; they danced about Terrence's head as the boys cruised through sagebrush country.

"I'll let you wipe the booger away if you'll let me take these boxers off."

Levi shook his head while a grin spread across his face. "A deal's a deal and the rules are the rules. The boxers stay put 'til day's end."

Terrence slumped in his seat. They didn't speak for over an hour. Meanwhile the day was heating up. Sweat beaded on Terrence's upper lip and the armpits of Levi's T-shirt grew dark.

When they were about halfway to San Antonio, Terrence straightened his spine. He pointed westward through the windshield. "What are those hills with the flat tops?"

"They're called mesas," Levi said.

"They look like someone sawed the peaks off them," Terrence said. "And are those real mountains way off in the distance?"

Levi squinted while he stared through the windshield at the western horizon, where brown masses loomed in the distance. Heat radiating off the highway's surface made them shimmer.

"They're mountains, all right," he said. "I mean, they're nothing like the Rockies or the Sierra Nevada, but they *are* mountains."

"Cool, but how do we get around them?"

"Through a pass."

"Imagine," Terrence said, "being pioneers in covered wagons and seeing those mountains for the first time. I'll bet they freaked out."

Levi nodded. "And just think: we're making this trip in five days. It would have taken them as long as six months to cross the country."

Terrence shook his head. "They must've wanted to reach California pretty badly."

"Well," Levi said, "don't you?"

Terrence looked at Levi and blinked his eyes. "Of course I do, or I wouldn't be here right now."

Levi returned his gaze to the highway. "Pioneer Terrence," he cried while pounding the steering wheel. "He's crossing the prairie in his Bo Peep van. Westward-ho and yippee tie-yi-*yay*."

Chapter Seven

LEVI AND TERRENCE reached the outskirts of San Antonio just around noon. The van's interior was hot, and both boys had shed their shirts. They found a shady rest stop with picnic tables where they ate their lunches, Levi with the booger stuck to his nose and Terrence wearing Levi's boxers on his head. People kept staring at Terrence when they passed him on their way from the parking lot to the restrooms; Terrence's cheeks flamed at their attentions, but when he begged Levi for permission to remove the boxers—even temporarily—Levi shook his head.

"They stay on until we go to sleep tonight," he said.

Terrence grimaced and shook his head. "You're a bit of a sadist, you know."

But Levi only chuckled.

Once they were back on the road, Levi used a bypass to avoid going through downtown San Antonio. Then they were back on I-10, zooming past towns like Boerne, Comfort, and Kerrville. The terrain was hilly and green, a nice change from what they'd encountered west of Houston, but still monotonous as hell.

"Isn't the Alamo around here somewhere?" Terrence asked.

Levi nodded. "Actually, we already passed it by; it's in downtown San Antonio."

Terrence made a face. "Did you say *downtown?* I saw a Disney movie about the Alamo once. I thought it was in the middle of a prairie."

"It probably was at one time," Levi said, "but not now. I actually stopped to see it back in May when I was driving to Florida. What a disappointment."

"Why?"

"It's a very small building with low walls, and it's surrounded by skyscrapers."

Terrence shook his head. "I guess life is like that: you have all these expectations, and then you get let down, over and over. It's like my job at Disney. I thought being inside the Magic Kingdom every day would be so cool, but then it turned out to be like any other job."

"Life's not *always* like that," Levi said. "Take Stanford, for instance: it's been everything I thought it would be, and maybe even more."

Terrence mopped his brow with his T-shirt. "I keep wondering how it's going to be, living in San Jose with Hseuh-Yu. I mean, I don't know anyone there but him, and I would guess the people in California are very different from those in Florida. They might not like me."

Levi crinkled his forehead. "What makes you say that?"

"I'm just a kid from Orlando who's never done much with his life."

Levi hissed and shook his head. He couldn't understand Terrence's utter lack of confidence. "Don't be so hard on yourself. You'll be okay."

"Do you really think so?"

Levi nodded. "You and I have only known each other for two days, but I'd say we're getting along well."

"True," Terrence said, "but then you're an easy person to like."

"Me?" Levi said, raising his eyebrows. Then he hissed again. "My family members would disagree. Mom's nickname for me is Sullen Sam. I think she's worried I'll spend my entire life alone, and she might have reason to."

"Why?"

Levi stared out the windshield. "I have Asperger's. Do you know what that is?"

"No."

"It's a mental syndrome that makes me unsociable. I find people hard to understand—I don't often know what they want from me—and so it seems easiest not to deal with them at all."

Terrence squirmed in his seat while he gathered his eyebrows. "But you have to *try*. The whole point of living is to find someone you can give yourself to completely. At least that's what my mom taught me, and I believe it. Otherwise, I wouldn't be moving to California."

Levi pondered Terrence's comment as they cruised in a northwesterly direction. If Terrence was right—and Levi suspected he might be—then it meant Levi had yet to grasp the very reason for his existence.

Am I walking around in a bubble?

They passed by Segovia, and when they reached the town of Junction, the road turned due west. They passed Roosevelt and then Sonora, a town of one-story structures and modest homes perched on hillsides. The wind passing through the van was arid, and by now, the booger on Levi's nose had dried up and blown away

Terrence shook his head as he stared out the passenger window. "What do you suppose people here *do* when they're not at work or school?"

Levi shook his head. "Maybe go to rodeos or hunt elk? Who knows, but I sure wouldn't live in a place like this."

Terrence shifted his weight in his seat. "What about you? When you're not studying at Stanford, what do you do with your free time?"

Levi thought for a moment before he answered. "I like to camp on the weekends, and I like to ride my mountain bike on trails around Palo Alto. Sometimes, I'll take the train into San Francisco. I just walk the city streets, checking out people and the architecture; it's fun."

"Do you do all those things alone?"

Levi nodded.

"Don't you have any friends?"

Levi pondered Terrence's question. How to explain? "Because of my Asperger's, I don't form social relationships like most folks do. Like I told you before, I do things by myself because it's easier for me that way."

Terrence crinkled his forehead. He gazed at his hands and twiddled his thumbs. Then he looked at Levi. "Now that you've told me something personal about you, maybe I should tell you something else personal about me. It's something only my grandparents know about."

"Sure," said Levi. "Go ahead."

"Not long after my mom died—I was fifteen then—I got in trouble with the law. A vacant house in our neighborhood had a shed in the backyard. One day, I set fire to the shed; it burned to the ground before the fire department could get there to put out the blaze."

Levi shook his head. "That doesn't sound like you."

Terrence shrugged. "Anyway, a neighbor saw me do it and called the cops. Then I was arrested and taken to juvie. I had to go to court with my grandparents. I got put on probation, which included mandatory counseling."

"What was *that* like?" Levi asked.

"Not so bad. I saw this lady once a week for a few months; we did a lot of talking. She said I had anger issues related to my mom's death and also because my dad had neglected me. And she said I suffered from low self-esteem, which was why I didn't have many friends."

Levi didn't say anything.

"She told me I should become more sociable and outgoing."

"Did you?"

Terrence shook his head. "It's easier said than done."

Just then the front of the van began to rumble and shake. Levi looked at Terrence and Terrence looked at Levi, both with puzzled expressions on their faces.

"Do you feel that?" Terrence said.

Levi nodded. "I'm pulling over."

Moments later, they were parked on the highway's shoulder. Levi knelt on the ground to examine the front tire on the van's passenger side while Terrence stood alongside him. The bottom of the tire was flat and the wheel it encased was almost flush with the ground. A roofing nail with a head the diameter of a quarter protruded from one of the tire's treads. The sun beat on Levi's shoulders and the top of his head. Sweat trickled down his ribs.

"Shit," he cried. "What lousy luck."

"Is it bad?" Terrence asked.

Levi looked at Terrence and nodded. "There's no way we can drive on it. We'll have to put your spare tire on."

"I'm not sure I even *have* a spare tire."

"Let's look," Levi said.

Terrence followed Levi to the van's rear, where Levi knelt and peeked under the rear bumper. Then he looked up at Terrence. "You've got one all right, and hopefully it has air in it."

Levi took a few minutes to locate the van's jack and lug wrench set. They rested in a recess inside the van. Both looked like they had never been used. Levi used two rocks he'd found on the roadside to chock the van's rear wheels. Then he removed the spare tire from its mounting underneath the van, getting himself filthy in the process.

"Get me a bottle of water, will you?" he said to Terrence. "I'm sweating like crazy."

Terrence did so, and Levi guzzled water like a draft animal while Terrence watched. Terrence still wore Levi's boxer shorts on his head and he was still shirtless.

He crossed his arms over his chest and asked Levi, "Do you think the spare will work?"

Levi poked the side of the spare with a thumb. "It feels pretty firm."

"Well *that's* good," Terrence said while he glanced here and there at the desolation surrounding them. There wasn't a building or even a power pole in sight, just hills and sagebrush and dirt. "For a minute there, I thought we might be walking back to Sonora."

After Levi drained the water bottle, he rolled the spare tire around to the front of the van. He located the insertion point for the jack's wrench-mounting bracket and popped off the hubcap on the flat tire's wheel, then loosened the wheel's lug nuts, one at a time. He put the pieces of the jack together: the base, the stand, the mounting bracket and the lug wrench, then jacked up the front right corner of the van. He sweated as he labored, and sunlight reflected off his shiny back.

"I wish there was something I could do to help you," Terrence said.

"You can get me another bottle of water," Levi said.

The corner of the van crept higher as Levi pumped the wrench and the jack's bracket creaked upward, one tick at a time. When Terrence returned with a bottle of water, Levi chugged the entire thing in thirty seconds.

"Thanks," he told Terrence while he smacked his lips.

"No," Terrence said. "Thank *you*."

Levi squinted. "What for?"

"If I had made this trip on my own and something like this happened, I don't know what I would have done. A wildcat might have eaten me."

After he'd handed Terrence the empty water bottle, Levi resumed jacking up the van until the flattened tire was separated from the ground. Then he started removing the wheel's lug nuts, one at a time. Each time a nut came off, he tossed it into the hubcap.

"Do you work out in a gym?" Terrence asked.

Levi made a face and shook his head. "Why?"

"I can see all the muscles in your back and shoulders. You look like one of those guys in a fitness magazine."

Levi shrugged.

"I'll bet all the girls like you," Terrence said. "You can probably have anyone you want."

Levi looked up from his efforts. "Taylor's only the second girl I've been with. I already told you about the first, and that was five years ago. Trust me. I'm not getting swarmed by women."

"Then how'd you end up dating Taylor?"

Levi shrugged. "She can be aggressive when she wants something. She came after me and I just let it happen."

Terrence shifted his weight from one leg to the other. "Maybe you *should* marry her."

Levi squinted while he shook his head. "She's too bossy, plus I want someone a lot more interesting. She can't see past the tip of her nose, if you know what I mean."

Terrence nodded while he chewed a hangnail. "I guess a lot of people would say I'm not too interesting either."

Levi stopped loosening a lug nut. He looked up at Terrence and pointed a finger. "Why are you always running yourself down? I mean, look at what you're doing right now: moving to California to start a new life and driving cross-country with a total stranger. A lot of people wouldn't have the courage."

"I'm only doing it because I *have* to," Terrence said. "If my grandparents weren't moving to the ALF, I'd still be playing clarinet at Disney."

"Maybe so," Levi said. "But you were faced with a problem, and now you're dealing with it in a very brave way. At least that's what I think."

Once Levi had removed all of the lug nuts from the wheel, he lifted the flat off the van and dropped it to the ground. Then, after he mounted the spare on the van, he began screwing the lug nuts back onto the wheel, using his grimy fingers.

"It is *so* stinking hot," he said. "I can't wait to jump into that swimming pool at the RV park."

"How many more hours do we have to go today?"

"Maybe two," Levi said while he kept working on the lug nuts. "We should make it to Fort Stockton by four at the latest. I'm so filthy and sweaty. The first thing I'll do is take a shower, and then we can hit the pool."

"I should tell you something," Terrence said.

"What's that?"

"I don't know how to swim."

Levi looked up at Terrence and grimaced. "You grew up in Florida, but never learned how?"

Terrence shook his head.

"I can't imagine," Levi said while he ratcheted the jack downward and the van's front passenger side descended. "I've been swimming since I was five. I took lessons at the Boys' Club on Merritt Island."

"I always meant to do that," Terrence said, "but somehow it never happened. So I guess I'll stay in the pool's shallow end. At least it'll cool me off."

When the van was fully lowered, Levi tightened the lug nuts on the spare tire and popped the hubcap back on the wheel. The spare seemed to handle the van's weight well—it wasn't bulging much—and if they made it to Fort Stockton in time, Levi told himself, perhaps they could find a garage to fix the flat.

Before he climbed into the driver's seat, Levi tried to clean his hands as best he could with water from a jug and paper towels, but the pads of his fingers and his cuticles were as black as tar. He sniffed one of his armpits and made a face while he climbed into the van.

"You'll have to forgive me," he told Terrence, "but right now I reek."

Terrence inhaled deeply. "I don't smell anything."

"If you got any closer to me, you would."

Terrence shrugged as Levi twisted the key in the ignition, and then the van's engine roared back to life.

Levi hollered, "Fort Stockton, here we come," and they were back on the road, passing mesas and low green hills. They sped by Ozona where a sign proclaimed the place was "The Biggest Little Town in the World." But there wasn't much to see other than a two-story courthouse, a high school, and a Dairy Queen.

They rode in silence for the longest time, and once again, Levi's thoughts turned to Taylor's pregnancy. Should he call her again that evening, or would that send her the wrong message? He didn't want her to think he was obsessing over the situation, or that she had him on the defensive. But he wanted to keep the pressure on her to seek an abortion.

How best to do that?

Levi wished he knew someone he could ask for advice on the situation, but there was no way he'd confide in his dad, and he wasn't quite sure how his older brother might react. To Levi's knowledge, no one in the McKane clan had ever sought an abortion. Babies were gifts to married couples, not something that happened by chance to a quiet boy lured into sex by a strong-willed girl.

When they reached Fort Stockton, the sun was still high in the sky and the temperature was still in the mid-nineties. The town was mostly one-story structures, save for a two-story dimpled-block courthouse and a Hampton Inn. In fact, the most notable feature of the town was an enormous statue of a roadrunner bird that stood at the town's eastern limit, adorned with a sign that said Welcome to Fort Stockton. The sign also identified the bird as Paisano Pete, World's Largest Roadrunner. Terrence cackled when he saw the statue. He even had Levi take a photo of it with his phone.

"You can e-mail it to me when we get to California," Terrence said.

Levi found a service station with a garage, where they filled the van's fuel tank and left the van's flat tire to be repaired. The station's owner, an old guy with a walrus mustache and a Texas drawl, assured Levi he'd have the tire ready by nine the next morning.

The RV park wasn't much to look at. Each site had a concrete pad, a fire pit with a grill, a picnic table, a water faucet, and an electrical hookup, but no shade trees or shrubbery. Two-thirds of the sites were empty. The proprietor was a middle-aged woman with a twang in her voice. Her gray hair was parted in the middle and woven into a pair of braids as thick as rattlesnakes. The braids reached to her waist. After Levi paid her, he parked the van in their assigned site. Then he hustled to the bathhouse with a towel draped over his shoulder and his toiletry bag under an arm.

He didn't even turn the hot water handle on when he showered. The cool, clean water pounding the back of his neck and sheeting down his limbs felt luxurious, and for the first time since the van's tire had gone flat, Levi felt human. He soaped his chest, back and limbs, and then his armpits and crotch. He let the shower sluice away the soap, and then he shampooed his hair while he hummed "Stairway to Heaven," his favorite of all the tunes Terrence had played since their trip had begun. Then he used a brush to scrub the grime out from under his fingernails.

After he toweled himself off, he put on a pair of swim trunks he'd brought to the bathhouse and then strolled back to the van, where shirtless Terrence sat at their picnic table, munching roasted peanuts. A pleasant breeze came from the west and ruffled the edges of the boxer shorts that still encircled Terrence's head.

"How was the shower?" Terrence asked.

"Like a dream. It feels so good to be clean again." Levi looked at the filthy shorts and shirt he held in his hand and shook his head. "I won't be able to wear these again, not 'til they're laundered."

Terrence changed into his swim trunks in the van. Then they walked over to the park's swimming pool with towels hanging from their necks. The pool wasn't much bigger than one you'd see at a modest residence in Merritt Island, but the water was sparkly and the furniture on the deck surrounding the pool looked new.

A girl and a boy who both looked to be kindergartners dawdled about the pool's shallow end, while two women in sundresses conversed at a table with an umbrella shading it. Levi tossed his towel onto a chaise, then dove into the pool's deep end, head-first, while Terrence entered the shallow end via the stairs. When Levi surfaced, he shook water from his face and treaded in the deep end as he watched Terrence submerge himself up to his neck for a few seconds before standing up straight again.

"Water feels good, doesn't it?" Levi said.

Terrence smiled and nodded. Droplets of pool water glistened on his shoulders. He pointed to the boxer shorts atop his head. "Can I at least take these off while we're here? I want to get my hair wet."

"Sure," Levi said, "you can do that."

Terrence went to the pool's edge and tossed the boxers onto a chaise, alongside his towel. Then he fully submerged himself for a few seconds before resurfacing. His dark hair was plastered to his skull and reflected the glow of the afternoon sun. He rubbed water from his eyes with his knuckles and looked at Levi with a grin on his face.

"This is great," he said. "Now, if only I could swim, everything would be perfect."

"I could teach you how," Levi said. "It's not that hard."

"Really?" Terrence said. "You mean right now?"

Levi nodded. Then he swam over to where Terrence stood. "Listen, swimming is all about learning how to float. You have to keep your lungs filled with air so that you're buoyant. The rest is all about learning different strokes: the freestyle, the breaststroke, and the sidestroke."

Levi took Terrence by his skinny bicep and positioned him so that he stood to Levi's right and facing away from Levi. "I'm going to hold my arms out in front of me, just below the water's surface. I want you to cross your arms at your chest. Then fall backward onto my arms so you're looking into the sky. Understand?"

Terrence looked at Levi from over his shoulder. "You won't drop me, will you?"

Levi shook his head. "You won't weigh much once you're floating."

Terrence swung his gaze away from Levi. He crossed his arms at his chest. Then, after he drew a deep breath, he let himself drop into Levi's grasp. Levi's left arm was underneath Terrence's shoulder blades while his right arm supported the backs of Terrence's knees. To Levi, Terrence felt as light as a potato chip. Terrence's chest rose and fell as he gazed into the afternoon sky.

"Okay," Levi said, "we'll practice floating. You're going to take a deep breath and hold it. Then I'll lower my arms just a little bit, so you can see how it feels to float. Got it?"

Terrence bobbed his chin.

"Ready?" Levi said.

Terrence nodded again. He inhaled deeply. Then Levi lowered his arms several inches so that he was no longer supporting Terrence's weight.

"How do you feel?" Levi said.

"Okay," Terrence said. "But it seems weird that I'm not sinking."

Levi let Terrence float for a few seconds more and then raised his arms until he was supporting Terrence again. After they'd repeated the exercise several times, Levi had Terrence stand up. Levi went to the pool's edge, where he rested his arms on the decking. Then he demonstrated flutter-kicking while Terrence watched with his arms folded at his chest.

The little kids in the pool stared at Levi as though they'd never seen anything so fascinating.

"You want to keep your feet moving so they'll propel you forward," Levi said. "Now you try doing it just like I am."

Terrence approached the pool's edge. He positioned himself as Levi had. He tried kicking but his feet kept sinking.

"You're not kicking rapidly enough," Levi said. "And you've got to keep your feet close to each other, not so far apart like you're doing right now. Try it again."

After five minutes of practicing, Terrence finally managed to keep his feet close to the water's surface when he kicked.

"Much better," Levi said. "You'll use that style of kick when you do the freestyle."

Terrence made a face. "What's a freestyle?"

"A style of swimming stroke you might see in the Olympics."

Terrence crinkled his nose. "I've never watched the Olympics."

Levi shook his head. It amazed him how little experience Terrence had with so many areas of life, as though Terrence had traveled through life ignoring much of his surroundings. Levi spent ten minutes teaching Terrence how to stroke his arms, one at a time, alternating left to right while Terrence stood chest-deep in the pool. After Terrence got the movement down to Levi's satisfaction, Levi demonstrated breathing head-turns by placing his face in the water, then turning it to the left to take a breath. He had Terrence perform the exercise over and over, letting him get used to having his face submerged.

"Exhale when your face is in the water. Then inhale when it's turned to the side and out of the water. Got it?"

They kept at it another five minutes or so. Then Levi said, "I'm going to hold my arms out in front of me like before. But *this* time you're going to lie on them face-down so you can practice kicking and stroking, and also breathing."

Terrence winced. "I'm not sure I can do all that at one time. It's a lot to remember."

"Give it a try," Levi said. "It's not as hard as you think."

Terrence ran a hand through his damp hair. "You promise you won't let me sink?"

"I promise. And look, we're only in waist-deep water; it's not like you could drown."

"All right," Terrence said. "Let's do it."

Moments later, Terrence lay atop Levi's arms. Levi's left arm supported Terrence's rib cage while his right supported Terrence's thighs. Droplets of pool water glistened on Terrence's shoulders, in his dark hair as well. He trembled all over.

"Quit shaking," Levi said. "There's nothing to be frightened about."

"I can't help it," Terrence said. "This is scary."

"I've got you," Levi said. "I won't let you sink. Now, let's get started: practice your flutter kick first."

Terrence made splish-splashy sounds as he kicked away at the water.

"Good," Levi said. "Now try stroking your arms while you kick. Remember to bend your elbows."

Terrence kicked and stroked, kicked and stroked. In the meantime, two girls in their late teens entered the pool deck through the chain-link gate. Both wore bikinis; they each carried a rolled-up towel under an arm. Their brown hair was parted in the middle and grew to their shoulders; they could easily have been sisters, except one girl was taller than the other by a few inches. They took chairs at an unoccupied table and shared a candy bar while staring at Levi and Terrence with bemused expressions on their faces.

Levi returned his attention to Terrence, who continued to stroke and kick. "Now try the breathing motion with your head," Levi said. "Put your face in the water. Exhale, and then turn your face to the left. When it's above water, you'll inhale."

Terrence did as he was told. He drew a breath about every three seconds while he kicked and stroked, kicked and stroked.

"Good job," Levi said. "Keep it up."

Terrence worked away for a good five minutes until Levi told him to stop. "I'm going to let go of you, and then I want you to stand up," Levi said.

It was only when Levi brushed his forearm across Terrence's groin area that he realized Terrence was sporting an erection in his swim trunks. Levi didn't want to embarrass Terrence, so he pretended not to notice the erection when Terrence slid from his arms.

"Well?" Terrence said, after planting his feet on the pool bottom. "How'd I do?"

"Really well," Levi said. "Let's take a break."

When the girls finished their candy bar, they tossed the wrapper and entered the pool via the steps at the shallow end, where they submerged themselves up to their necks in the cool water. They weren't more than fifteen feet from Levi and Terrence.

The taller girl spoke to Levi in a syrupy voice that was flavored with a Texas drawl. "How's the lesson going?"

"Good, I think," Levi said, "considering it's his first time."

"I'm Janice," the girl said and then pointed to her companion. "She's my friend Krystal."

Levi introduced himself and Terrence and explained their travel plans.

"California?" Janice said. "I've never been, but I'd love to go one day, maybe see Hollywood and meet a movie star."

Levi shook his head. "Go to San Diego instead or head north to San Francisco; you'll like it much better there."

The girls were from Dallas, traveling with Janice's parents to Albuquerque where they would visit Janice's aunt and uncle. Janice pointed to a shiny RV the size of a city bus; it was parked at a campsite not that far from the one Terrence and Levi occupied.

"We've been riding in that thing for two solid days," she said, "and all the time, we have to listen to Daddy's country-western music. If I hear one more Big & Rich tune, I think I'll lose my mind."

Both Janice and Krystal had just graduated high school. They would attend Southern Methodist University as incoming freshmen at the month's end. "I'm good at science," Janice said. "I plan to become a dentist or an orthodontist; I hear those jobs pay well."

Levi spoke briefly about Stanford and his scholarship, as much as he could without feeling self-conscious.

"You must be pretty smart," Krystal said. "I hear Stanford's a good school."

All the while, Terrence said nothing. His gaze traveled from person to person as each spoke. He was chewing a hangnail when Janice turned to him and puckered one side of her face.

"Don't you know how to talk?" she said.

"He's a little shy," Levi said before Terrence could answer, "but he plays wicked clarinet; you should hear him."

Terrence's cheeks colored; he didn't say anything in response to Levi's remarks.

"I was in marching band at my high school," Krystal told Terrence. "I play flute."

"Nice," Terrence managed to say.

"You're cute," Janice said to Terrence. "How old are you, anyway?"

"Guess," Terrence said.

Levi winced because he knew what was about to happen.

"Sixteen?" Janice said.

Terrence lowered his gaze while his entire face turned as red as a brick. Then he worked his jaw from side to side.

"He's *nine*teen," Levi said. "He just looks young for his age."

"Oops," Janice said while she hunched her shoulders. Her gaze traveled from Krystal to Levi, then to Terrence. "I didn't mean to make you feel bad."

When Terrence looked up, his eyes were glistening. "It's okay. Everybody thinks I'm younger than I am."

"Well," Janice said to Terrence, "you're still cute." Then she turned to Krystal. "Don't you agree?"

Krystal bobbed her chin, and Terrence blushed anew.

Levi thought back to his discussion with Terrence that afternoon, just before the van's tire went flat. They had both acknowledged the importance of being more sociable, and here was an opportunity to do just that.

"Listen," Levi said to Janice, "Terrence and I need to go get our dinner going in a few minutes, but later on, why don't we all get together?" He pointed to the Bo Peep van. "That's our site over there if you want to visit."

Janice glanced at Krystal before she returned her gaze to Levi.

"We'll see," she said.

Chapter Eight

BACK AT THEIR campsite, Terrence sat at their picnic table, watching Levi core and slice an apple. The sun was low in the western sky and a pleasant breeze fluttered the legs on Levi's boxer shorts that once again perched on Terrence's head. The boys had already pitched Levi's tent and laid out their sleeping bags inside, and now they sipped from cans of beer while they talked.

"I think those girls liked you," Terrence said.

Levi shrugged as he carved seeds out of an apple slice. "*You're* the one they said was cute, not me."

Terrence shook his head. "They only said that to make me feel better after, you know...."

"Look," Levi said while he pointed his knife at Terrence's nose, "that was your fault; you set yourself up by asking Janice to guess your age."

Terrence didn't say anything; he only chewed a hangnail.

When Levi finished carving up the apple, he sliced half a cheddar cheese block into wedges. He placed those on a paper plate, alongside the apple slices, and brought out a box of wheat crackers. He sat across the table from Terrence and the two snacked while they talked about the next day.

"Tucson's 550 miles from here," Levi said, "about an eight-hour drive. If we leave here by nine tomorrow morning, we'll get there by 5:00 p.m. at the latest."

Terrence chewed on an apple slice. After he swallowed, he asked Levi, "When do you think we'll make it to San Jose?"

"I'm thinking Tuesday night or midday Wednesday, depending on traffic in the L.A. area."

"This trip's going by so fast," Terrence said. "It feels like we only left Florida yesterday."

Levi nodded. "Are you feeling nervous about meeting your friend?"

"*Very* nervous," Terrence said while he rearranged his limbs. "I'm not really sure what to expect of Hsueh-Yu, or what he expects of me."

"You two haven't discussed that sort of thing?"

Terrence shook his head.

Levi tried to imagine himself in Terrence's position. Terrence would be entirely dependent on the new boyfriend for housing, food, and everything else. Plus, he wouldn't know a soul in San Jose.

"I wish this trip would take longer," Terrence said. "I'm actually enjoying myself. Are you?"

Levi shrugged. "Aside from the flat tire business, sure. Travel's always interested me, even if it means driving through west Texas. Plus..."

"What?"

Levi's gaze met Terrence's. "You're...good company. This is much better than making the trip by myself."

Terrence's cheeks reddened while he placed a cheese wedge onto a cracker. He popped the cracker into his mouth and munched with a contented expression on his face.

After he swallowed, he asked Levi, "Have you ever seen the Golden Gate Bridge?"

Levi looked at Terrence like Terrence was nuts. "Dozens of times; I even walked across it."

Terrence's eyebrows jumped. "Weren't you scared?"

Levi shook his head. "There are fences to keep you from falling; it's totally safe. And the views of the bay and the city are amazing. You should get your friend to take you sometime soon."

When the snack plate was empty, Levi tossed the plate and busied himself with preparing a meal both he and Terrence could share. At a supermarket in Fort Stockton, he had purchased tempeh, a carrot, an onion, and fresh garlic, and now, after he'd diced up all the veggies and tempeh, he sautéed them in olive oil over a low flame. After he'd put water on to boil for spaghetti noodles, he added marinara sauce to the veggies and tempeh.

"That smells great," Terrence said after he'd drained his second beer. "You're sure you don't mind a meatless meal?"

Levi shrugged. "I'll be fine, plus it seems kind of silly for us to eat separately, don't you think?"

Terrence nodded.

Levi gave Terrence a knife and a cutting board. Then he handed Terrence a head of iceberg lettuce and a tomato. "Make us two salads. Cut the tomato into wedges, and then tear leaves off the lettuce head;

break the leaves into bite-size pieces." He handed Terrence two paper bowls. "Put them all in these."

Terrence got to work on the salads. He kept licking one corner of his mouth as he did so. Already the sky was darkening and shadows had grown long. Levi lit his propane lantern, which made a pleasant hissing sound while the mantles glowed. People occupying RVs and campers in the park began switching on lights. Probably half the sites in the park were in use.

After Levi added spaghetti noodles to the pot of boiling water, he went about setting the table for dinner: paper plates, silverware, and paper napkins. He uncorked a bottle of Chianti, produced two plastic wineglasses.

Terrence reached for the wine bottle and inspected the label as though it offered the key to solving a mystery. "Is this stuff any good?"

Levi shrugged. "We paid nine bucks for it, so it should be okay."

"I've never drunk wine," Terrence said. "What's it taste like, grape juice?"

"It's not sweet at all," Levi said while he stirred the noodles in the bubbling pot. "In fact, it's very dry but goes well with pasta and red sauce. You'll like it, I think, if you'll give it a chance."

When the noodles were done, Levi drained the water from the pot. Then he divvied up the cooked noodles onto the plates. He spooned the tempeh sauce over the noodles and brought out a bottle of Italian dressing for the salads. The food on the plates steamed as the boys sat opposite each other at the table. After Levi poured wine into the glasses, he raised his toward Terrence.

"A toast to our journey."

Terrence touched the rim of his glass to Levi's. After he took a tentative sip of wine, he made a face like he'd swallowed medicine. "It's more bitter than beer."

Levi poured dressing over his salad. "It'll taste better, once you've had a few bites of your food."

Terrence ate two forkfuls of salad. Then he sampled the spaghetti. "It's good. You'll have to give me the recipe so I can make it for Hsueh-Yu."

"Is he vegetarian?"

Terrence shrugged. "How would I know?"

Levi crinkled his forehead. "Exactly how many times have you *spoken* with this guy?"

Terrence twirled his fork, gathering noodles around the tines. "Maybe ten, but most of our conversations have been short. He's not much of a talker, at least not on the phone."

Levi raised an eyebrow while he chewed on a mouthful of salad. The lettuce made crunching sounds inside his head as he pondered what Terrence had just said. The more Terrence revealed about his dearth of interaction with the San Jose man, the clearer it became to Levi that Terrence's odyssey to California was little more than a crap shoot.

By the time the meal was finished, Terrence had drained his wineglass and his speech sounded a bit slurred. "That was one of the best dinners I've ever had," he told Levi. "Who taught you how to do this?"

"My mom," Levi said. "She's the best damn cook in Brevard County, has an herb garden and everything."

Terrence lowered his gaze for a moment before he returned it to Levi's. "Can I share something else personal with you?"

"Sure, go ahead."

Terrence poked his sternum with a fingertip. "Ever since *my* mom died, I've felt like I have a hole in my heart that will never heal. Sometimes I get so lonely I want to jump off a bridge."

Levi felt his throat constrict. "You were that close to her?"

Terrence nodded. "We were best friends, really. We did everything together, like watching TV and going to movies. She loved the shore, so we used to drive over to Cocoa Beach at least twice a month. We'd stay at a hotel and eat out in restaurants; it was so cool."

"Did you ever tell her?"

"What?"

"That you're gay."

Terrence shook his head. "I was only fifteen when she died. I didn't identify myself as gay at the time."

"When *did* you know?" Levi asked.

"Oh, I always knew, at least in the back of my mind. But I just didn't want to admit it, not 'til I was sixteen. I got this huge crush on a boy who sat next to me in my Spanish class. Every day, I couldn't wait 'til fourth period rolled around so I could hear his voice and look at him."

"Did you ever tell *him?*"

Terrence shook his head again. "Like I said before, I've kept it a secret from everyone I know. But it feels good to talk with you about it; I think you're someone I can trust."

Levi lowered his gaze to the tabletop. He didn't know exactly what to say, but he felt very good about Terrence confiding in him. It was a new experience for Levi.

Terrence rose. He gathered the dirty silverware and pots into Levi's dishpan and left for the bathhouse to clean everything up. Levi was sitting by himself, staring up at the night sky, when Janice and Krystal appeared from out of the darkness. Both wore skimpy halter tops, denim shorts, and sandals.

"Mind if we join you?" Janice said while she stared at the Bo Peep van like it was a vessel from outer space.

"Have a seat," Levi said. He hadn't counted on the girls even showing up, but now they had. He motioned them to the bench across the table from him. Then, after they sat, Levi asked if they drank beer.

When Janice looked at Krystal, Krystal shrugged. Janice returned her gaze to Levi. "Sure," she said, "we'll both have one."

Moments later, both girls sipped from cans while Levi asked questions about SMU.

"I wanted to go to Sam Houston State, in Huntsville," Janice said, "just to put some distance between me and my folks. I told them, 'Look at all the money you'll save on tuition if I go to a state school.' But Daddy wouldn't hear of it; he wants me close by."

Krystal rolled her eyes. "Both my parents are SMU grads; they *never* miss a home football game, and my mom's still involved with the Tri-Delt house on campus, so there's no question where *I'm* going to school."

Just then, Terrence appeared with Levi's dishpan under an arm and the front of his T-shirt soaked with water.

When the girls saw him, Janice pointed to Levi's boxer shorts on top of Terrence's head. "Why are you wearing those like that?"

Terrence blushed while he lowered his gaze.

"They're mine," Levi said. "We were playing Truth or Dare this morning, and I decided to get creative. He has to wear them 'til we go to bed tonight."

Both girls giggled while Terrence stowed the dishpan and the items he'd cleaned inside the van. Then he joined Levi on the bench Levi occupied.

Janice pointed at Levi and asked Terrence, "What did you dare *him* to do? I hope it was something just as stupid."

"You don't want to know," Levi said before Terrence could answer. "It was totally disgusting."

Terrence snickered while his gaze traveled from the girls to Levi. "It *was* pretty gross, wasn't it?"

"Okay," Janice said, "now you guys *have* to tell us. Come on, out with it."

Levi rolled his eyes and shook his head while Terrence told Janice, "I stuck a fresh booger on the tip of his nose."

"Yuck," Krystal cried. "Did you really do that?"

Terrence grinned while he nodded. Janice made a face like she'd sucked on a kumquat. "Now I don't feel so sorry for you," she told Terrence. "No *wonder* he made you wear those on your head."

Terrence didn't respond. Instead, he poured himself a fresh glassful of Chianti. After he took a sip, he smacked his lips and rearranged his limbs. "Want me to play some music?"

"Sure," Levi said.

Moments later, Terrence was assembling his clarinet while the girls and Levi watched, and Levi found himself wondering whether or not the girls noticed how chewed up Terrence's fingernails were. When Terrence finished his work, he wetted his reed and played a few scales. The pleasant-sounding notes wafted through the warm evening air.

Krystal said, "My band teacher always called clarinets 'licorice sticks,' I guess because of the way they look. But maybe because of the way they sound: kind of seductive and sweet."

Terrence looked at Krystal; he nodded and said, "I'm going to play 'Over the Rainbow' from *The Wizard of Oz*." And then he did.

Levi closed his eyes. *The Wizard of Oz* had been his favorite movie when he was a boy; he must've watched it thirty times when he was seven and eight years old. He had memorized the words to all the songs in the film, and now, as he closed his eyes, he could see Judy Garland in her twin ponytails and jumper dress, singing "Over the Rainbow" while clinging to a wagon wheel. He recalled a Halloween when he'd trick-or-treated as the Scarecrow.

When Terrence finished "Over the Rainbow," everyone clapped, even an elderly couple sitting in lawn chairs in a nearby campsite. Terrence stood and bowed at the waist with a smile on his lips.

After he sat, he said, "Now I'm going to play the theme from *Jurassic Park*."

"Cool," Krystal said. "I love that song."

A chill ran down Levi's spine while Terrence played the majestic tune. Terrence had perfected the piece to the point that he knew exactly when to increase the volume at each crescendo. The RV park's manager rode up on a beach cruiser bicycle and stopped to listen to Terrence play. She fiddled with one of her braids while the glow from Levi's propane lantern reflected in her ice-blue eyes.

More applause erupted when Terrence finished the song. Someone in another campsite whistled through his teeth while Terrence blushed and waved.

"Play 'Stairway to Heaven,'" Levi said to Terrence when the applause died down. "You know that's my favorite."

"You know 'Stairway'?" Krystal asked Terrence.

"Of course. Why?"

"Let me get my flute; it's in the RV. Then we can play a duet."

Krystal was back in three minutes with a hasped case that looked similar to Terrence's, only slimmer. The silver instrument rested in the case in three pieces that Krystal quickly assembled. After she raised the flute to her lips, she moistened them and played a few scales. The notes sounded like whispers to Levi as Krystal worked the keypads with her fingertips.

After Krystal had warmed up, she looked at Terrence. "It's in A-minor, right?"

"That's correct," Terrence said. "Are you ready?"

When Krystal nodded, Terrence said, "On four." Then he counted to three out loud before bringing his clarinet's mouthpiece to his lips.

Levi shivered as the duet began. It seemed to him as though the sounds the two instruments produced were intertwining like a pair of mating snakes. The music poured out of the clarinet and flute like syrup. Levi stole a glance at Janice. Her brown-eyed gaze was fixed on Terrence; she studied his fingers as Terrence tickled the clarinet's keypads. She sipped her beer, licked her lips.

I'll bet she has a rich boyfriend, Levi told himself. *Girls like her usually do.*

More applause and whistling exploded when Terrence and Krystal finished "Stairway." Terrence grinned at Krystal before he sipped his wine and then asked her if she knew how to play Bette Midler's "Wind Beneath My Wings."

Krystal nodded. "C-major, right?"

Terrence nodded, and seconds later, they launched into the tune. While they played, Levi pulled three fresh beers from his ice cooler. He placed them on the picnic table—one in front of himself, the others before Janice and Krystal—then opened his. He was feeling about as relaxed as he'd ever been, just listening to the music while enjoying the girls' presence and savoring the cold crispness of the beer. What could be better?

When the song ended and the ensuing applause finally died, Terrence said to no one in particular, "I think that's enough from me for tonight."

"Oh-h-h," Janice said. "You guys sound so good together. I could listen for hours."

"Thank you," the park manager cried out before she pedaled away with her braids fluttering.

"You're welcome," Terrence called out to her, and Levi wondered if Terrence had ever received so much attention from so many people at one time. Terrence's visage seemed to *glow* as he disassembled his clarinet. Then he placed the pieces in their designated recesses in his case.

"You're awfully good," Krystal said to him while she took apart her flute. "How long have you played?"

Terrence explained. Then he talked about his audition with the symphony in San Jose. "It pays much better than my old job at Disney. I guess because there's a lot of money in Silicon Valley right now."

"I'll bet you'd look real cute onstage in a tux," Janice said.

Terrence lowered his gaze while his cheeks colored.

"Why are you blushing?" Krystal said to Terrence. "She was only giving you a compliment."

Terrence looked at Krystal and shrugged. "I'm not used to getting compliments from girls."

Janice drained her first beer and cracked open the new one that rested on the table before her. "I have an idea," she said, looking at Levi. "Why don't the four of us play Truth or Dare? It'll be fun."

Levi raised a shoulder, let it drop.

"I don't know," Terrence said while he pointed to his head and scowled. "Look what the last game earned me."

"Krystal and I won't be nearly as cruel as you guys were in your game," Janice said. "We'll keep it nice, I promise."

Krystal squinted while she cracked open a fresh beer. "Come on," she said to Terrence. "You can even go first."

Terrence stuck his hands between his knees while he worked his jaw from side to side. Then he looked at Levi. "What do you think?"

"Why not?" Levi said. "We don't have anything better to do."

"Okay," Terrence said. He pointed a finger at Janice. "Truth: What's the biggest secret you hide from your parents? I mean the one you'll never, ever tell them about."

Janice puckered one side of her face while her gaze flitted from face to face in the lamplight. She took a sip from her beer and swallowed noisily. She tucked a hank of hair behind her ear, and after she stole a quick glance at her family's RV, she answered.

"Our senior class trip was a cruise from Galveston to Cozumel and back. On the ship, I met a Mexican boy named Cristobal; he was a crew member and really cute. We ended up, you know...."

"What?" Terrence said.

"Messing around in the cabin I shared with Krystal."

"No," Terrence said.

Janice nodded while her gaze swung to Levi and then Krystal before she returned it to Terrence. "We didn't go *too* far, but if Daddy found out I even kissed that boy, he'd throw a fit. He doesn't like Mexicans; he'd probably disown me if I ever dated one."

"Truth," Janice said, pointing at Terrence. "Tell us about the first time you tongue-kissed a girl."

Terrence's face turned as pale as an egg while he looked into Janice's eyes and blinked. He swung his gaze to Levi and then looked at Janice again. After he cleared his throat, he told her, "I've never kissed a girl, tongue or no tongue."

Janice crinkled her forehead. She glanced at Krystal and returned her gaze to Terrence. "But you're nineteen. How is that possible?"

"I'm gay," Terrence said. "I'm not attracted to females, so why would I kiss one?"

Right away, things at the table grew very quiet; the only sound Levi heard was the hiss of his propane lantern. Both girls stared at the tabletop.

Janice crossed her arms beneath her breasts. After thirty seconds or so, she looked up at Terrence. "I didn't mean to embarrass you like that. I just assumed you were...."

"Straight?"

Janice nodded.

"Sorry to disappoint you," Terrence said.

"I'm not disappointed," Janice said. "You just took me by surprise."

"I have a gay friend from school," Krystal said. "His name's Paolo; he's from Brazil. The girls are all crazy about him 'cause he's so sexy—you should see his smile—but of course, they never get anywhere with him."

Levi knew that Krystal and Janice were trying to make Terrence feel better about himself, but their efforts struck Levi as condescending and he didn't like that. "Are we still playing Truth or Dare? We seem to be straying off course."

"I'll go next," Krystal said, and pointed at Levi. "Truth: when is the last time you let someone see your penis?"

Everyone at the table, including Levi, burst into laughter.

"What kind of a crazy question is that?" Levi asked Krystal.

"Go ahead," Janice said. "You know the rules; you have to answer, and your answer has to be truthful."

Levi turned down one corner of his mouth while he shook his head. Then he pointed at Terrence. "It was him just this morning."

Krystal's eyebrows jumped while Terrence giggled. Krystal's gaze flitted between Levi and Terrence. "Exactly what were you two doing when this happened?"

Levi rolled his eyes. "Don't get too excited. I took my boxers off in the van so Terrence could put them on his head."

"You wouldn't believe this guy," Terrence said to Krystal while pointing at Levi. "He doesn't care *who* sees him naked."

Levi shrugged and turned to Krystal. "Truth: who's the last person who saw *you* naked?"

Laughter erupted around the table again. Krystal's gaze traveled to the night sky while she pursed her lips and slumped her shoulders. "I'll need a minute to try to remember 'cause I think it's been a while."

"Take your time," Levi said with a grin on his face.

Krystal glanced at Janice and then said to Levi, "I remember now. And this is embarrassing...."

"Go ahead," Levi said.

"I was at a pool party last summer. It was nighttime, at a girl's house; her parents were out of town. Kids were drinking and smoking weed, the usual high school stuff."

"Okay...."

"Anyway, I was in a bathroom getting out of my swimsuit so I could put on dry clothes, and I guess I forgot to lock the door. This kid—he couldn't have been older than fourteen—walked in on me when I didn't have a stitch on. I don't know who was more shocked, him or me."

Another round of laughter exploded. By now, Levi had finished his fifth beer of the evening and he was buzzed. Everything around him—the girls, Terrence, the van, and the tent—seemed to glow in the light cast by the propane lantern. And most everything anyone at the table said was humorous. The girls and Terrence appeared more relaxed than they had been at the time of the girls' arrival. Their shoulders sagged and their voices had a bit of a slur to them when they spoke. The beer and wine were clearly working their magic on everyone present.

When Terrence rose to his feet, he nearly lost his balance. He pointed at Janice and said, "My turn, and this one's a dare. I dare you to tongue-kiss Levi for a full minute, right here at the table."

Levi felt a twitch in his belly while Janice arched her eyebrows and her jaw sagged. Her gaze traveled from face to face. Then she looked at Terrence and said, "You're kidding, right?"

Terrence shook his head while his lips pulled back from his normally sparkling teeth that were now stained light purple by the wine he'd drunk.

Janice turned to Krystal as though she might have a lifeline available, but Krystal only shrugged and shook her head. Then Janice looked at Levi and puckered one side of her face.

"I guess I don't have a choice, now do I?"

Levi rose, albeit unsteadily, and his knees crackled when he did so. He kept his gaze fixed on Janice as he approached and sat beside her on the bench she and Krystal occupied. He felt tension sizzle between himself and Janice. After all, Janice was no Taylor. A true Texas beauty from a well-to-do family, she was the kind of girl most guys would have considered untouchable at Merritt Island High School.

Levi thought of his first time with Taylor, when she'd taught him proper kissing techniques.

"You're not doing this with your grandma," she told him. "Rub your tongue against mine and put some energy into it."

Now, Levi brought his hand to the nape of Janice's neck. "Are you ready?"

"Hold it," Terrence said while he raised his wrist to look at his watch. "Ready, set and...*go.*"

Levi brought his lips to Janice's—he felt her breath on his face—but when he tried to pry her lips apart with his tongue, Janice drew back and scowled.

"When's the last time you shaved? Your whiskers are like sandpaper."

"I'm not in high school," Levi said while he rubbed his jaw with the heel of his hand. "College men have stubble."

Janice shifted her buttocks on the bench and leaned toward Levi with her eyes closed. Again, Levi seized the nape of her neck. He brought his lips to hers and this time, succeeded in prying hers apart. After Levi slipped his tongue inside her mouth, Janice's breath steamed Levi's upper lip while his tongue rubbed against hers. The only sound at the table was the hiss of Levi's lantern and the smacking of their lips.

Levi was certain Janice would pull away after thirty seconds or so, but she didn't. She just kept on slobbering until Terrence hollered, "Time's up."

"Thank *god,*" Janice said while making a face and wiping her lips with the back of her hand.

"Was it that bad?" Levi asked.

Janice pointed to her chin. "You scratched me all up, bubba."

Terrence giggled like a schoolgirl. The red wine was gone from the bottle, and Levi was pretty sure Terrence was drunk because Terrence's speech sounded sloppy when he spoke. "I'll bet you *enjoyed* the kiss," he said to Janice. "You just don't want to admit it, do you?"

Janice growled and shook her head. Then she pointed at Terrence. "Here's a dare for *you*, Mr. Clarinet. Why don't *you* try kissing your pal, and let's see if *you* like it."

Levi's scalp prickled. "Hey...."

Janice wagged a finger at Levi. "I did what Terrence dared me to. Now you two have to do the same."

Krystal cackled while Terrence and Levi looked at each other.

"Come on," Krystal cried. "Get to it, guys, and we want to see plenty of tongue."

"That's right," Janice said. "And the kiss has to last a full minute."

Levi was too tired and drunk to argue with the girls. He looked at Terrence and shrugged while moving back to the bench where Terrence sat. After his hip touched Terrence's, he placed a hand on the back of Terrence's neck while Terrence gazed into Levi's eyes and blinked.

"Ready?" Levi said.

Terrence nodded.

"Hold it," Janice said. "Give me your wristwatch so I can time you guys."

After Terrence passed Janice the watch, she studied the dial for a moment and said, "Ready, set...*go.*"

Levi pulled Terrence's face to his and brought his mouth to Terrence's. He closed his eyes and pried Terrence's lips apart so he could probe the inside of Terrence's mouth with his tongue. Terrence's breathing quickened while his tongue dueled with Levi's. They made smacking sounds as they traded spit, and another shiver ran through Levi when he realized he'd grown stiff between his legs.

Moments later, when Levi and Terrence separated, Terrence's face was flushed. His chest rose and fell and his eyes looked glittery, like he was high on some sort of narcotic. Levi's spit gleamed on his lips.

Terrence kept his gaze fixed on Levi. "You're a lot better kisser than that guy at Disney," he said. Then he looked at Janice. "I didn't mind the stubble at all; in fact, I liked it."

A grin crept onto Levi's face. After he ruffled Terrence's hair, he looked at Krystal, then Janice. "Are you girls satisfied?"

Neither Janice nor Krystal said a word; they only stared at Levi like he'd just committed some sort of heinous crime, and it was then Levi realized the girls had never believed Levi and Terrence would actually take Janice up on her dare.

Levi rose and yawned deeply. He was tired of the game and tired of the girls too. He said to no one in particular, "I'm ready for bed." Then he gazed down at Terrence, who still looked a little dazed from their kiss. "How about you? Want to hit the tent?"

Terrence didn't speak, only nodded.

When Janice and Krystal rose, both seemed unsteady on their feet. Krystal picked up her flute case and looked down at Terrence. "Good luck in California. I hope you get the symphony job."

Terrence made a little smile.

"It's been an *interesting* visit," Janice said while she adjusted her halter top. "You boys have a good night now."

Levi and Terrence visited the campground's men's room to use the toilets. Then they returned to their campsite, where Levi extinguished the propane lantern and stowed it in the van along with his ice cooler. The time was close to 10:00 p.m.; most folks in the surrounding campsites had already gone to bed. Crickets chirped in nearby trees as Terrence scooted inside the tent. Levi followed and zipped the tent flaps closed. Nearby, a campground streetlight cast a glow that offered faint illumination inside the tent.

The boys undressed without speaking. Terrence removed the boxer shorts he had worn on his head all day but didn't return the boxers to Levi. Instead, he placed them on his pillow. The night was warm, and both guys lay atop their sleeping bags, staring up at the tent's ceiling and breathing.

Terrence wove his fingers together behind his neck. "I don't think they believed we'd actually kiss. I guess it freaked them out when we did."

Levi shrugged. "Served them right; they shouldn't have dared us."

"Did it bother you? The kiss, I mean?"

"I was fine with it."

"Am I the first boy you've ever kissed?"

Levi grunted. "Do you think I'd normally do something like that?"

Terrence turned onto his side so he faced Levi. He bent an elbow, rested the side of his face on the palm of his hand. After he moistened his lips, he said, "Is it okay if I tell you that I enjoyed our kiss *and* that I think you're kind of amazing?"

Levi's brain roiled. What should he say?

"Look, the kiss was okay. And the girls were right—you're nice-looking in your own way—but...."

"What?"

"You should probably save those feelings for your friend in San Jose."

Terrence rolled onto his back. Again, he interlaced his fingers behind his neck while he spoke. "Sex and love get complicated, don't they?"

"In what way?"

"Nobody seems to want the same thing. I'm attracted to you, but you don't like me that way. Taylor wants to marry you, but you aren't interested. You seemed to like kissing Janice, but she didn't like kissing you. And if you had dared me to kiss Krystal tonight, I wouldn't have—no way—even though any straight guy would have jumped at the chance."

Levi yawned while he shifted his hips on his sleeping bag.

"It's the way life works, I suppose. That stuff you read about in books—where two strangers randomly meet and then fall in love—is probably bullshit. I don't think it ever happens that way."

Chapter Nine

SUNDAY MORNING, LEVI woke to the sound of a diesel engine's rattle and a muffler's roar. He lay on his back, blinking as he stared at the tent ceiling. Then he glanced at Terrence, who slept on his side, facing Levi. Terrence's cheek rested on Levi's boxer shorts.

Levi shook Terrence's shoulder. "Time to get up."

Terrence's eyelids opened, and he groaned. "My head hurts."

"Mine does too," Levi said. "It's called a hangover."

Janice's RV was already gone by the time Levi and Terrence exited the tent. The boys visited the men's room and returned to their campsite, where they ate breakfast cereal. Levi's coffeepot gurgled on the propane stove. The sky was overcast. Off in the distance, thunder rumbled while a breeze stirred the branches of a nearby scrub oak.

Levi sniffed the air and detected the metallic scent of approaching rain, but wasn't concerned about the possibility of encountering showers that day. In fact, he welcomed the possibility of rainfall since it would keep things cooler on their drive to Tucson. And at least the storm had not arrived in the middle of the night. Their tent and the rest of the camping equipment were still dry.

They passed a plastic jug of orange juice back and forth, drinking directly from the jug as they talked about the day ahead. Terrence guzzled juice. After he swallowed, he wiped his lips with the back of his hand and asked Levi, "Ever been to Tucson?"

Levi nodded. "It's a good-sized city, but there's not much to look at really."

Terrence asked where they'd camp that night.

"I did an Internet search on my phone; I found another RV park east of the city. It has a swimming pool and a coin laundry. A tent camping site is only fifteen bucks per night."

The coffeepot had finished percolating, and now Levi filled two coffee mugs for himself and Terrence. Like always, Terrence dumped three spoonfuls of sugar into his mug, along with a dash of milk. Then he pursed his lips and blew into the mug to cool his coffee.

Levi scratched his chin and asked Terrence, "Do you think I should shave this morning? Am I starting to look like a bum?"

"You look fine," Terrence said. "Did it bother you what Janice said about your stubble?"

Levi shrugged.

"Like I told you last night," Terrence said, "your stubble didn't bother me when we kissed. In fact, I thought it was kind of sexy."

Levi rolled his eyes.

Terrence chuckled. "I can't believe the whole thing happened. I must have been buzzed off that red wine—it made me feel dizzy—and then when you kissed me...."

"What?"

"I thought I might pass out."

Levi felt heat in his cheeks. A boy had never said such things to him before. On one hand, he felt flattered, but on the other, he felt guilty, as though their kiss and his ensuing erection were things he should be ashamed of. He'd never gotten intimate with a boy before—he had never *considered* doing so—but now he'd done it with Terrence, and would that somehow change the dynamic between the two of them in the days ahead?

A half hour later, they stopped at the garage in Fort Stockton where the guy with the walrus mustache charged them ten bucks for fixing the flat. He even remounted the rejuvenated tire in the rack underneath the van's rear, so Levi wouldn't have to get dirty and sweaty doing so. Then they were on their way.

When they passed by the giant roadrunner at the edge of town, Terrence waved at the statue. "So long, Paisano Pete," he cried, and Levi steered the van onto the entrance ramp leading to I-10. Already, raindrops appeared on the van's windshield and a breeze stirred the sagebrush on either side of the highway. Thunder rumbled from time to time. Levi switched on the wipers and headlights as rain began to drum against the van's roof and windshield. Both of them rolled up their windows to keep the rain out, and they cruised in silence for a bit. The only sounds were the wipers clacking and the hum of the van's tires on the rain-slicked highway.

Terrence kicked off his Converse sneakers, put his bare feet on the dashboard, and chewed a hangnail. The land to either side of them was flat, other than the occasional mesa, but off in the distance, Levi saw mountains that looked to him like piles of dirty laundry.

"Have you talked with Taylor lately?" Terrence said.

"Not since Friday night, back in Houston. I don't want to call her too often, or she'll think I'm dwelling on the pregnancy. The more she thinks I don't care about the baby, the better."

"Do you really not care?"

Levi rocked his head from side to side while he steered into the inside lane in order to pass a slow-moving eighteen-wheeler. "Under different circumstances, I *would* care. I mean, if Taylor was someone I wanted to marry, and if I were finished with school, and *if* the pregnancy was planned, then I'd care—I'd care a lot—but that's not how things are."

They passed the semi, and then Levi steered the van back into the outside lane. They cruised at seventy-five miles per hour as they talked.

"If she has the baby," Terrence said, "and then goes after you for child support, what'll you do?"

Levi pursed his lips and shook his head. "I'm fucked. Unless my parents pay the support for a few years—and I doubt they would—I'll have to quit school and get a job."

"*That* doesn't sound too promising," Terrence said. "You should buy lottery tickets every week. Maybe you'll win some money; then you can stay in school and support the baby at the same time."

Levi looked at Terrence like Terrence was crazy. "The lottery? You're joking, right?"

Terrence shrugged. "A few years ago, a Bo Peep customer won a hundred thousand dollars on a scratch-off ticket he bought in Winter Park."

Levi shook his head again. "I don't think the lottery's going to save me. My only hope is she'll have an abortion, but as each day passes, I'd say the chances for that grow less."

By now the rainstorm had lessened to almost nothing, and Levi switched off the wipers. Both boys opened their windows to let fresh air in. The sky was still overcast, the color of dirty dishwater. The land they encountered was nothing more than sagebrush and low hills, most all of it was a monotonous shade of brown. They passed by one-story towns like Saragosa and Van Horn where the only modern buildings were low-end chain motels, and Levi could not imagine how anyone could stand to live in such places. A sign offered a twenty-acre site for $15,950, but what could a guy do with twenty acres of sagebrush? You couldn't even graze cattle on the Texas hardpan, could you?

From a box behind the driver's seat, Terrence retrieved his zippered money bag. He counted his cash while wind rushing through the van ruffled his hair. Then he looked at Levi with his eyebrows raised.

"I've only spent a third of what I thought I would at this point in the trip. You were right. Camping's the way to go when you travel."

Levi looked at Terrence and nodded. "Maybe you ought to buy yourself a tent and cook stove when you get to San Jose. They might come in handy one day."

Terrence squinted. "I'm not sure I could camp on my own."

"But it's not that hard," Levi said.

Terrence shifted in his seat. "It wouldn't be the same as doing it with you. It's like we're a team, do you know what I mean?"

"Yeah, but maybe your boyfriend will go camping with you. There are lots of cool places to visit in Northern California, like Yosemite and Lake Tahoe. They all have campsites."

Terrence puckered one side of his face and shook his head. "I'm not sure he'd like camping."

Levi stared out the windshield. The overcast sky gave the terrain around them a washed-out look. They approached an eighteen-wheeler from behind; it spewed water from the roadbed onto the van's windshield, forcing Levi to turn the wipers back on. He moved the van to the inside lane and then accelerated past the truck.

Terrence's phone rang. After he dug the phone from his pocket, he pushed the Talk button, and a conversation ensued.

"We're still in west Texas," Terrence said, "but we should reach Tucson by five or so.

"Yeah, pretty good, except we had a flat tire yesterday. Levi put the spare on and then we got the flat fixed at a garage.

"I *know* it's taking a lot of time, but we're traveling a long distance. I'm doing the best I can.

Terrence wagged a knee back and forth while listening to his caller. "All right, then," he said. "I'll call you from Tucson tonight."

When the conversation ended, Terrence took a deep breath and exhaled noisily. He shoved his phone back into his pocket and cracked his knuckles.

"Sounds like someone's getting impatient," Levi said.

Terrence looked at Levi and rolled his eyes. "He says we ought to be in Los Angeles already. He asked me if we were *sightseeing* along the way."

Levi snorted and shook his head. "We've already traveled over 1600 miles. What more does he want?"

"He's just anxious to see me. I think he's a bit lonely."

Levi shifted his buttocks. "I'm curious. Will each of you have defined roles when you're living together?"

Terrence crinkled his forehead. "Roles?"

"Yeah, like who will keep house and who will do yard work, that kind of stuff."

"We haven't discussed those things yet," Terrence said. "I'm sure we'll divide up responsibilities after I settle in."

"Do you think he expects to be the decision-maker because he's older than you?"

Terrence shrugged. "If he wants it that way, I'm okay with it."

"Really?"

"Yeah, why not?"

"Because you're an adult; you're entitled to make certain decisions for yourself, especially if you get a job and help pay the household expenses."

Terrence didn't say anything in response, and they rode in silence for the longest time, until they reached Fort Hancock. Levi's calf muscles were cramping like crazy, likely due, he thought, to all the time he'd spent behind the wheel the past three days.

"I'm going to stop and stretch my legs," he told Terrence while he steered onto an exit ramp. "And I could use something cold to drink. I've got a dry mouth from all the beer I drank last night."

Fort Hancock wasn't much. A border control office and the local high school seemed to be the largest structures in town. They found a convenience store where Levi performed several deep-knee bends in the parking lot, trying to relieve the tightness in his legs. After he'd loosened up, he and Terrence entered the store, which wasn't much either. A Mexican man sat behind the register, smoking a cigarette and watching a soccer match on a small television. The TV announcer spoke in Spanish.

Levi bought himself a soda and a bag of crushed ice for the cooler. Terrence chose a bottle of apple juice. When they exited the store, a boy with a backpack and a sleeping bag was climbing down from the bed of a pickup truck with a Texas license plate on it. The truck's cab was occupied by two men in straw cowboy hats. Once the boy's feet hit the ground, he waved to the men in the truck, and then they drove away with their muffler growling.

While Levi and Terrence climbed into the van, the boy, who looked to be in his mid-teens, approached the van's passenger door window. He fingered the shoulder straps on his backpack as he peered in at Terrence and Levi.

"Hey, guys," he said in a raspy tenor flavored by a Texas drawl. "Mind if I ask where you're headed?"

After Levi explained, the boy said, "I need a lift to Phoenix. Could you help me out?"

Levi and Terrence exchanged glances. Levi shrugged, and Terrence looked at the boy through the window. He jerked a thumb toward the rear of the van. "There aren't any seats back there, but you can sit on the floor if you'd like."

"The floor's fine," the boy said, and moments later he was seated behind Terrence, leaning against his sleeping bag with his knees raised and his forearms resting on them. "I'm Jacob," he told Levi and Terrence.

While they rolled down the highway, Levi looked at Jacob's reflection in the van's rearview mirror. The boy was lanky with long brown hair he'd parted in the middle of his scalp and tucked behind his ears; it grew well past his shoulders. His nose came to a point, his eyes were coffee-colored, and a few pimples dotted his cheeks. He wore a T-shirt with a Grateful Dead logo on the chest, faded blue jeans, and skateboarder sneakers. A leather bracelet encircled his wrist.

"What takes you to Phoenix?" Levi asked him.

"I'm visiting my dad."

"Where's home?" Levi asked.

"Austin," Jacob said. "I just finished my first year at UT, back in June."

Jacob's response took Levi by surprise because Jacob didn't look college-age to Levi, but Levi reminded himself that Terrence didn't look nineteen either. After Jacob fished a water canteen out of his backpack, he took sips from it. Then he smacked his lips.

"How many days have you been on the road?" Levi asked him.

"Just yesterday and today," Jacob said. "Last night, I slept in an abandoned building outside of Sheffield. Coyotes howled all night long, and this morning I saw a rattlesnake as big as my arm. I can't say as I care for west Texas."

"And I thought *we* were roughing it," Terrence said to Levi.

"Did you have anything to eat today?" Levi asked Jacob.

When Jacob said no, Levi pointed to his ice cooler. "There's lunch meat, cheese, and mayo in there, and a loaf of bread and silverware are in that cardboard box next to you. Make yourself a sandwich."

"Thanks," Jacob said, "thanks very much." And then he got busy preparing the sandwich. While he worked he said, "This is my first hitchhiking experience. I guess I didn't plan things out too well."

Terrence turned in his seat to look at Jacob. "Weren't you frightened when you heard those coyotes last night?"

Jacob looked up from a slice of bread he was slathering with mayonnaise. "I was *real* scared. I didn't sleep a wink; I just lay there in my bag and wondered if I might get eaten before dawn came."

A few minutes passed and then Levi said to Jacob, "What kind of courses did you take at UT last school year?"

"Oh, the usual stuff: English, math and, let's see...astronomy."

Levi made a face while he stared out the windshield. *Freshmen don't study astronomy, and a UT student wouldn't hitchhike alone in west Texas.*

After Jacob constructed his sandwich, he carefully returned the food items to the ice cooler and the cardboard box. Then he ate the entire sandwich in less than two minutes, smacking and gulping like a wolf devouring a lamb.

"You must've been hungry," Terrence said while Jacob licked his fingers clean.

Jacob looked at Terrence and nodded. "I haven't eaten since yesterday morning."

After Levi and Terrence exchanged puzzled glances, Levi asked Jacob, "What's your dad do for a living in Phoenix?"

"My dad? He's...an airline pilot; he flies jets for Delta."

Levi looked at Jacob's reflection in the rearview again. "How come he didn't have Delta fly you to Phoenix? Austin has an airport, doesn't it?"

After Jacob lowered his gaze, he studied his shoes for a moment. Then he looked up at Levi's reflection in the rearview. "He doesn't know I'm coming for a visit; I want to surprise him."

Now Levi *knew* the kid was spinning tales.

The three boys rode in silence for a while. Then snoring noises came from behind Levi. When he turned to look at Jacob, the boy was fast asleep. Jacob's chin rested on his chest and his arms were crossed on his stomach. A string of saliva dangled from one corner of his mouth.

Levi looked at Terrence and shook his head. "Poor guy must've been exhausted from last night."

Terrence glanced at Jacob and spoke in whispers to Levi. "I don't get it. What's he doing in the middle of nowhere with no place to sleep and no food?"

"I don't know," Levi whispered back, "but he's not telling us the truth about himself—I'm certain of that. He's no college student and his dad's not a Delta pilot either."

"How do you know?"

"I just do."

Terrence looked at Jacob again, shook his head, and turned back to face the windshield. After he'd placed his feet on the dashboard, he stared out the windshield at the monotonous terrain they passed through. It was mostly sagebrush, low hills, and mesas. A dead bighorn sheep lay on the road shoulder. Its beefy hindquarters were mangled, Levi presumed by collision with a large vehicle, probably an eighteen-wheeler.

By now the sky had cleared and sunlight baked the roadbed. The van was heating up, and both Terrence and Levi rolled down their windows so fresh air could enter. Terrence's dark hair fluttered about his face while he stared out the passenger door's window.

"So," he said, "what kind of job can you get with a Forestry degree?"

"All different kinds," Levi answered. "I could work for a paper company, helping manage their land. Or I could work for the US Forestry Service or the federal park service, or also a state park service might hire me."

"Do any of those jobs pay well?"

Levi shifted his weight in his seat. "Not really, but they'd allow me to work outdoors by myself most of the time, and that's something I'd like to do. I don't want a job in an office cubicle where I have to deal with people all day."

"If I *did* go to college, I'd study music," Terrence said. "Maybe I could become a band teacher at a high school."

"Hey, why not?" Levi said.

Terrence rocked his head from side to side. "I'm not sure I'm smart enough for college."

Levi grimaced. "There you go again—running yourself down. You seem pretty bright to me. How were your grades in high school?"

Terrence shrugged. "I made Honor Roll each term; I did okay."

"San Jose State's a good university. Even if you get the job with the symphony, you could still attend part-time."

"I'll talk with Hseuh-Yu about it. I'll see what he thinks."

Levi grunted. "It's not like you need his permission to go to school. That's a decision *you* should make on your own; it's your life, not his."

Terrence shrugged again, and the conversation ceased. They rode in silence for a long while. The only noise inside the van was Jacob's snoring. A little past noon, they reached El Paso, a good-sized city with several high-rise office buildings and a huge brown mountain looming over it. Using his cell phone, Levi located a lakefront park not far from I-10 and exited the highway.

Once at street level, they passed a shopping mall, a home improvement center, and several fast food restaurants. Then, after Levi turned off the thoroughfare, they drove through a subdivision of two-story homes that all looked brand new. Most were painted in shades of tan or brown; many had decorative stone accents. All had gravel yards and only a few homes had trees. None had their windows open.

Levi shook his head. The subdivision's barrenness depressed him. "Water must be scarce around here. Nobody has grass in their yard."

But the park Levi had located was pretty, with twisting live oaks and several picnic shelters overlooking a lake with Muscovy ducks swimming on its surface. After Levi parked, he turned toward Jacob and shook the boy's shoulder. "Wake up. We're stopping for lunch."

Jacob's eyelids fluttered open, and he looked around him as though he didn't know where he was. He yawned deeply, scratched his head. "How long was I asleep?"

"Maybe an hour and a half," Levi said. "I think you needed rest."

Jacob nodded. "Where are we?"

After Levi explained, he exited the van and stretched his limbs like a housecat. He rubbed his belly and flexed his toes while Terrence went to the van's rear doors and opened both. Jacob crawled out, and then Terrence brought the ice cooler to a nearby picnic shelter. Only a few families were in the park, people with little kids playing on the jungle gym. Levi toted the cardboard food box over to the picnic shelter as well, and then all three boys sat around the table. A pleasant breeze blew and the shade provided by the shelter made things comfortable.

"Would you like another sandwich?" Levi asked Jacob.

"I don't want to eat up all your food."

"It's fine," Levi said. "We have plenty."

"All right then, sure."

Levi set about making two sandwiches while Terrence brought out cheese, peanut butter, and his milk jug. He cut up an apple on a paper plate and then offered slices to Levi and Jacob.

Jacob munched while his gaze traveled here and there. A fistful of hair had fallen into his face and he tucked it back behind his ear while he chewed.

After he swallowed, he asked Levi, "I like this park; how'd you find it?"

Levi pulled his cell phone out of his pocket and handed it to Jacob. "The GPS makes it easy to find whatever kind of place you want: parks, restaurants, campgrounds, you name it."

Jacob gazed at the phone screen and shook his head while he handed the phone back to Levi. "I wouldn't know how to use it."

"You don't have one?"

Jacob shook his head.

"Ask your dad to put you on his phone plan," Levi said. "It won't cost him much."

Jacob didn't say anything, he only shrugged, and again Levi wondered what Jacob's true story was. Didn't *everybody* Jacob's age have a cell phone?

After Levi handed Jacob a sandwich, Terrence poured milk into a plastic glass and handed it to Jacob.

Jacob said, "You guys are really kind to give me food. I only expected a ride and nothing more."

"What were you planning to eat on this trip?" Levi asked. "You knew it would take at least three days, right?"

Jacob lowered his gaze and then looked back at Levi. "Like I said, I didn't think things through very well before I hit the road. All I cared about was getting to Phoenix."

Levi watched Jacob gobble his sandwich. As before, the whole sandwich disappeared within two minutes. Jacob drained his glass of milk, and when Terrence offered him another apple slice, he didn't hesitate to take one.

"So," Jacob said in between munches, "are you guys on vacation?"

Levi shook his head. Then he explained the purpose of his and Terrence's journey. "This is our fourth day on the road. With any luck, we'll reach northern California by midday Wednesday."

Jacob licked apple juice from his fingers. Then he asked Levi, "How far do you guys plan on traveling today?"

"We're going to Tucson," Levi said. "We have a campsite reserved in an RV park. If you want you can stay there with us, you can sleep in the van, and then we'll drop you off in Phoenix tomorrow."

Jacob glanced back and forth between Levi and Terrence. "You guys wouldn't mind?"

Levi shook his head.

Then Terrence said, "The van's not the most comfortable place to sleep, but it sure beats coyotes and rattlesnakes."

"Thanks, guys," Jacob said. "You're the nicest people I've met in like...forever."

Chapter Ten

TWO HOURS LATER, they stopped to fill the van's fuel tank at an exit leading to the town of Deming, New Mexico. The terrain surrounding them differed from that of west Texas: less sagebrush, more cacti. And the mountains in the distance were craggier and steeper than those they had previously encountered. The sky seemed a brighter blue as well.

They took turns using the men's room at the gas station/convenience store, and during his turn, Levi took the time to wash his face with cool water in the men's room sink. He studied his visage in the wall mirror after he did so. His stubble gave him a swarthy appearance, and he wondered if perhaps he should shave soon. But then he recalled how Terrence had said he *liked* Levi's stubble, so maybe shaving *wasn't* necessary.

Back on the road, they passed any number of one-story towns where the most significant structures were high schools and courthouses: Gage, Wilna, and Separ. Conversation ceased; the only sound inside the van was wind rushing in through the windows. Jacob had fallen asleep again not long after they'd left Deming, but this time he wasn't snoring. He lay on the van's metal floor with his legs outstretched and his head resting on his bedroll. In the passenger seat, Terrence read a graphic novel titled *Maus*, authored by Art Spiegelman, a book Levi had seen kids reading back at Merritt Island High. The cover featured a swastika and a cat's face with Hitler-like features.

Levi had never read a graphic novel—he considered them nothing more than glorified comic books—but a lot of kids he knew liked them. "Is that book any good?"

Terrence looked at Levi and nodded. "It's about the Holocaust during the Second World War. Do you know much about it?"

Levi shrugged. "I know the Nazis murdered something like six million Jews, mostly in gas chambers."

"It must've been a terrible time," Terrence said. "Death and more death."

Levi rubbed his chin with a knuckle. Then he asked Terrence, "Do you think abortion is murder? Is it immoral?"

After Terrence dog-eared the page he was reading from, he put the book aside. He looked at Levi and then turned his gaze to the windshield before he answered. "It's a difficult question, isn't it? Is a two-month-old fetus a living person or not? I mean, who knows?"

"I'll tell you what I think," Levi said. "The worst choice Taylor could make would be to have this baby she's carrying. It'll mess up my life, hers, and the baby's as well. Even if I have to quit school and pay child support, I'm not going to marry Taylor, so the kid will grow up with no father in its life. How is that a good thing?"

Terrence brushed his bangs out of his eyes. "I totally get what you're saying. A kid needs two parents. I think if my dad had stuck around when I was growing up, I would be a more confident person than I am today. A boy needs his father, day in and day out." Terrence jerked a thumb in Jacob's direction, and then he spoke in a whisper. "I guess he needs his dad right now, 'cause he sure wants to get to Phoenix in a hurry."

Levi glanced over his shoulder at Jacob. Then he shook his head.

"What is it?" Terrence asked.

Levi returned his gaze to the windshield and spoke in a low tone. "I don't think much of what he's told us is true. None of it adds up."

Terrence raised an eyebrow. "What do you think his real story is?"

"I don't know," Levi said. "It could be anything."

"But he seems nice enough," Terrence said.

Levi shrugged, and his thoughts returned to Taylor. What exactly should he say to her tonight? Should he take an aggressive approach or a sympathetic one? He knew Taylor well enough to know she would not be intimidated. If she felt backed into a corner, she'd get obstinate, and that would only make matters worse.

In the passenger seat, Terrence re-opened his book and read. His lips moved silently as he mouthed the words he read. His dark hair fluttered about his face. They rode in silence for an hour or more, through desert-like terrain where the most common color was brown and cacti thickets abounded. Jagged mountains rose in the distance. They passed Lordsburg, where a sign said the town's elevation was 4,250 feet, a statistic that surprised Levi.

Another thousand feet and we'd be a mile high.

They entered Arizona, and when they reached a town called Wilcox half an hour later, Levi exited I-10 to park at a rest stop and stretch his legs. The afternoon sun pounded his shoulders and the crown of his head while he walked to the restrooms and drank from a water fountain. The water tasted a bit sulfurous, but at least it wasn't warm. When he returned to the van, Terrence was munching on handfuls of roasted peanuts and chasing them with bottled water. His book rested in his lap.

"How much farther 'til Tucson?" he asked after Levi fired up the van's engine.

"Maybe ninety minutes." Levi backed the van out of its parking space. "We should be there by four, I'm guessing."

"If there's time," Terrence said, "I'd like to visit the city for a little while, just to see it."

"We can do that," Levi said, "but don't expect too much."

"You have to remember something," Terrence said. "This is my first real travel adventure, so *everything* I'm seeing is special to me. Aren't *you* having fun?"

Levi raised a shoulder and let it drop. "I am, but this situation with Taylor keeps dogging me. I wish I could get things resolved."

Terrence wiped sweat off his forehead with the back of his forearm. "There's not much you can do but wait and see what she chooses."

Levi didn't respond to Terrence's observation, but he knew Terrence was right. The situation was out of his control. He felt like a mouse getting toyed with by a cat. *Stop thinking about it,* he told himself. *Put it out of your mind.* But he couldn't, so he stared out the windshield and pondered the fact that seven months from now he'd likely be back in Brevard County, doing tune-ups at his dad's garage.

Some of the land west of Wilcox was cultivated. They passed a vineyard and a wheat field. They even saw a golf course. Off in the distance, craggy brown mountains thrust their peaks into the cloudless sky that was a brilliant shade of blue. But ten minutes later, they were back in sagebrush and cacti country, and Levi found himself longing for the coastal beauty of Brevard County or the lush landscapes of Palo Alto.

Tucson sat in a valley surrounded by mountain ranges. I-10 snaked through a pass in the Rincon range east of town. They traveled between two walls of rock for a time. Then, once they entered the valley, Levi had to use the van's visor to ward off the sun's glare that poured through the windshield and hammered the dashboard. Levi's T-shirt was damp in the armpits and stuck to his chest and the small of his back. Terrence had already shed his shirt. He drummed his fingers on the sill of the passenger door. Off in the distance, the city's skyline appeared, a half dozen nondescript high-rises that reminded Levi of inverted ice cube trays. He checked the location of the RV park, using the GPS on his phone.

"Are you sure you want to drive into town?" he asked Terrence. "The exit to our park is coming up."

Terrence twisted in his seat. "This may be the only chance I'll ever get to see Tucson."

"Okay," Levi said, "if you really want to." And so they kept driving westward, past low-slung residential subdivisions, shopping plazas, and car dealerships, until they reached the exit to central Tucson. Then they descended to street level.

Even downtown, most commercial structures were one- or two-storied and nondescript. Homes were squatty, either brick or mission style, and none had grass. Their yards were simply dirt the color of bran flakes, dotted here and there with thirsty-looking shrubs. Most trees appeared stunted. The only tall ones were Italian pines, Washingtonia palms, and the occasional eucalyptus. Commercial streets were lined with small businesses: takeaway Tex-Mex, tattoo parlors, tire stores, motels, and fast food chains. Few people roamed the sidewalks because the day was simply too hot for outdoor activity of any kind.

They cruised the city's broad avenues, first on East Congress Street, which gave way to East Broadway. The tallest buildings cast long shadows. Levi turned left, onto North Park Avenue, and then they reached the Arizona University campus, which Levi thought was the town's most impressive institution. The buildings were contemporary, mostly red brick and glass. A football stadium existed for the Wildcats, who played in the Pac-Twelve Conference. But even on campus, there was not much grass, save for one treeless plaza; it sat unused and out of place, amidst all the brownness.

Terrence looked here and there and then told Levi, "I don't think I'd like living here. It's hotter than Orlando, and where are the trees?"

Levi snickered and said, "Let's check out the foothills; I hear they're nice compared to town."

They drove northeastward for a dozen miles, and then the land began to rise toward the Santa Catalina mountain range. They passed two country clubs; the fairways there were green but only barely, with yellow patches here and there. Homes in the area were mostly two-story adobe-style structures. Vegetation was lusher than in town. No grass grew, but many trees did—mesquite mainly—to a dozen feet or more. Levi saw pines and aspens as well. And everywhere saguaro cacti grew, the kind of multi-branched monsters he'd seen in cowboy movies and read about in a botany class at Stanford.

He pointed to one that must have been fifteen feet tall, a monster with multiple arms. "A cactus like that can live 150 years or more."

"You're kidding?" Terrence said while he stared at the cactus and shook his head.

The road became a series of switchbacks as they continued to climb and the van's engine chugged. A sign they came to told them a "scenic outlook" was 500 feet ahead, and when they reached the turnout, Levi parked the van in a small asphalt lot with a few tire stops and a set of coin-operated binoculars on a pedestal.

Behind Levi's seat, Jacob stirred. He sat upright and stretched his arms while he yawned. "Where are we? And what time is it?"

After Levi explained, Terrence said, "Let's get out and have a look at the view."

All three scrambled from the van; they stood at the parking lot's edge, staring down at the city below them. The downtown buildings seemed much smaller when viewed from a distance. Levi's gaze traveled over the grounds of a resort; its swimming pool glittered like a mirror. One of the golf courses they'd passed on their way up looked like an oasis among all the brownness surrounding its emerald fairways. Here and there, adobe-style homes perched on hillsides, while above them jagged peaks that looked like tombstones thrust into the sky.

"I wonder what it's like here in winter," Terrence said while visoring his eyes with a hand held to his brow. "Do you think it snows?"

Levi shook his head. "You'd have to go to a higher elevation for that."

"Does it cost a lot to live in a place like this?" Jacob asked, looking at Levi.

"I'm sure," Levi said, "'cause it's so much nicer than town. But still, it's so damned hot up here I don't know how people stand it. I say we head for the RV park; I'm ready for that swimming pool."

Moments later, Levi used the van's lower gears as a brake when they descended to the valley. The time was nearing five p.m., and traffic thickened as they drove at street level toward I-10. Before they hit the interstate, they visited a supermarket to buy food, along with more ice and a twelve-pack of beer.

Levi bought eggs, ham slices, grated cheddar cheese, and a green bell pepper. "I'll fix omelets for tonight's dinner," he told Terrence. "I can leave the ham out of yours."

Jacob bought himself a can of beef stew. He fished three dollar bills out of a wallet that wasn't much thicker than a pancake.

The RV park was much like the one in Ft. Stockton. A dozen RVs and a few tents occupied sites shaded by mesquite trees. A pair of coin-operated washers and dryers stood outside a bathhouse. The swimming pool and pool deck were surrounded by a chain-link fence. The office was an A-frame with a shaded front porch and plate-glass windows. A roan-colored pony stood tethered to a hitching post out front, also shaded by a mesquite tree. The pony's ears twitched when Levi patted its neck before entering the air-conditioned office where an old guy in a suede cowboy hat and a checkered shirt sat behind the counter.

After Levi paid for a tent-camping site, he traded the old guy a few dollars for quarters to operate the laundry equipment. Then he parked the van in their assigned space, which was nothing more than a patch of dirt with a water spigot and a picnic table. But a mesquite tree offered shade, and an afternoon breeze stirred the tree's spindly branches.

Once he'd pitched his tent, Levi placed the sleeping bags and pillows inside it. Then he told Terrence, "I'm going to wash my dirty clothes before we swim. Do you have anything you want laundered?"

Terrence nodded. Then he pawed through a cardboard box in the van, removing underwear and shirts he'd worn since the trip began. He gave these to Levi, who stuffed them into a pillowcase along with his dirty items. Then Levi headed for the bathhouse, where he bought a box of detergent from a wall-mounted dispenser. Moments later, a washing machine was chugging and Levi returned to the campsite. Terrence and Jacob had already changed into swimming attire. Terrence wore his swimsuit, while Jacob wore a pair of cotton gym shorts. Jacob was as skinny as Terrence, with stringy muscles on his frame. A pink two-inch scar resembling a centipede showed on his shoulder.

Levi climbed into the van, where he wriggled out of his clothes and into his swimsuit, and then the boys ambled to the park's swimming pool with towels hanging around their necks.

The pool water looked a bit murky and the bottom was littered with pine needles, but Levi didn't care; he dove into the pool's deep end. The water felt deliciously cool as he rose to the surface and shook droplets off his face. He treaded water while he watched Jacob and Terrence descend the pool stairs, looking like a pair of scarecrows who'd lost most of their clothing.

Jacob slid beneath the water's surface and swam the length of the pool underwater before emerging next to the diving board. He looked at Levi and grinned. "Water feels great." He swam back to the pool's shallow end, again underwater, stroking with his arms and flutter-kicking while his long hair fanned out above his shoulders.

When Jacob surfaced by the pool stairs, Terrence looked at him and clucked his tongue. "You're a good swimmer. Where'd you learn?"

Jacob pulled a wet strand of hair from his face and tucked it behind an ear. "There's a city pool not far from the house I grew up in. They gave lessons to kids for free during summer."

"Levi's teaching me to swim," Terrence said, looking at Levi. "Can we do it again today?"

"Sure," said Levi, who hung by his arms from the diving board. "Why don't you start by practicing your flutter kicks?"

Terrence moved to one edge of the pool, where he folded his arms on the ledge and rested his chin on them. He began kicking his feet, making splashy noises while Jacob and Levi watched.

"A little faster," Levi said, and Terrence picked up the pace. Water flew here and there as Terrence chugged his feet. This went on for a few minutes until Terrence's breath huffed and his face was flushed.

"That's enough. Take a rest." Levi swam over to Terrence, who stood in waist-high water with his hands on his hips.

Terrence's chest rose and fell as he gulped air into his lungs. "It's hard work, keeping my feet near the surface."

"True," Levi said, "but when you're floating and stroking your arms, it gets a lot easier. You'll see."

Levi gripped Terrence's bicep and turned Terrence so he stood to Levi's right, facing Jacob, who sat on the pool steps, half submerged. "I'm going to hold my arms out in front of me like I did yesterday. Then you lie across them like before."

Terrence followed Levi's instructions. He wriggled into position so that Levi's left arm supported Terrence's rib cage while Levi's right arm supported Terrence's thighs. As before, Terrence seemed as light as a pool float to Levi.

"Practice your head-turns and breathing while you stroke your arms and kick your feet," Levi said.

Terrence did so. He'd lower his face to the water for a few seconds, then turn his head to the side to breathe. At the same time, he pawed the water with his hands and flutter-kicked. His dark hair was plastered to his skull, and water droplets glistened on his skin.

After a minute or so, Levi told Terrence, "I'm going to let go of you, and then you'll swim toward Jacob, understand?"

"Okay," Terrence hollered when he turned his head to the side.

Levi lowered his arms, and Terrence moved toward the pool's shallow end in a herky-jerky fashion. He made it halfway to Jacob before his feet descended to the pool bottom, and he stood up straight, spitting out water and shaking his head.

"How come I sank?" he asked Levi.

"You weren't stroking your arms fast enough," Levi said. "Let's try it again."

They did so, over and over, until after fifteen minutes, Terrence made it all the way to the pool steps without sinking. He rose to his feet with a grin on his face while water sheeted from his skin.

Jacob and Levi clapped their hands, and Levi let out a war whoop. "You're a swimmer now."

"Well," Terrence said, "not exactly a swimmer, but it's a start, isn't it?"

Levi nodded. "Practice some more on your own. You don't need me holding you anymore; just swim from one side of the pool to the other until you're comfortable with it."

While Terrence chopped and kicked away, Levi joined Jacob on the pool steps. By now, the sun was low in the western sky and the shadows around them had grown long. A family of campers—two parents with a boy and a girl in tow—walked past them, carrying towels and toiletry kits and heading for the bathhouse. Neither child looked older than six or seven to Levi.

"How's the water?" the mom asked.

Levi flashed a thumbs-up. "Nice and cool." He lowered himself onto the pool's lowest step so that he was submerged up to his shoulders.

Jacob ran his fingers through his damp hair while he kept his gaze on Terrence's back-and-forth movements. "This school you go to in California," he said to Levi. "What's it called?"

"Stanford. You haven't heard of it?"

Jacob shook his head. "Do you like it there?"

"A lot," Levi said. "And Palo Alto's a beautiful spot to live in. How's UT?"

Jacob shrugged. "Okay, I guess."

"Any idea what you'll major in?"

Jacob shrugged again. "I'm thinking I might want to be an animal doctor. What are they called?"

"Veterinarians," Levi said. "It's a tough course of study: lots of biology and chemistry classes, that sort of thing."

"I like animals," Jacob said. "I always wanted to have a dog like a German shepherd or a collie, but my parents wouldn't let me. The best I ever got was a hamster that ran on a wheel, but he died after only a few months."

"So," Levi said, "I guess your mom and dad don't live together?"

Jacob shook his head. "They're divorced. I live with my mom in Austin; we have an apartment near campus. Mom's a…nurse at a hospital."

More bullshit, Levi told himself. Then he told Jacob, "I'm going to grab a can of beer from the van; I'll be right back."

Moments later, Levi pawed through the contents of Jacob's backpack, most of it T-shirts, socks, and underwear that were faded and/or stained. But when Levi unzipped a small pocket near the backpack's lower edge, he found was he was looking for: a lanyard with a plastic student ID from Round Rock High School clipped to it. The ID included a headshot photo of Jacob and his date of birth.

Jacob Fournier had turned sixteen two weeks before.

Levi fingered the edge of the ID while he studied Jacob's photo. Then he reached for his cell phone. After a quick Internet search, he learned that Round Rock was a town on the northeastern edge of Austin. The town's website made Round Rock sound like a desirable and growing place, with good schools and public services. A second Internet search reflected only a few Round Rock residents with the last name Fournier. One was a female CPA, another was James Fournier, a guy who'd been arrested by the Williamson County Sheriff's Department several times on minor offenses. A third person, Zachary Fournier, had recently died and left no survivors.

An Internet search on Jacob Fournier yielded nothing.

After he returned the ID and lanyard to Jacob's backpack, Levi toted two cans of beer back to the pool, where he found Jacob and Terrence chatting at the pool's shallow end. Terrence was talking about his former job at Disney World while Jacob listened intently, as though Terrence's life in Orlando must have been terribly fascinating.

Levi tapped Terrence on the shoulder, interrupting the conversation, and then Levi handed Terrence a beer. "I thought you might want this."

Terrence nodded while he cracked open the can.

Jacob licked his lips while he watched Terrence sip from the can. Then he looked at Levi. "Are you twenty-one?"

Levi shook his head.

"Then how do you guys get away with buying beer?"

Terrence giggled. Then he told Jacob, "Levi has a fake ID; it says he's twenty-two."

Go on, Levi told himself, *you should confront the kid now.*

"Speaking of IDs...," Levi said, staring at Jacob.

Jacob looked at Levi and crinkled his forehead. "What?"

"I just looked at yours in your backpack. Why don't you tell us what life is like at Round Rock High School?"

Jacob lowered his gaze while his cheeks turned crimson. He worked his jaw from side to side while he stared into the pool water.

Terrence looked at Levi and squinted. "What are you talking about?"

"I'll let Jacob explain that," Levi answered. After he opened his own beer, he took a healthy swig. The beer was so cold it numbed the back of his throat when he swallowed but in a good way.

Jacob kept his gaze lowered. "You shouldn't have gone through my things—not without asking."

"And you shouldn't be telling us stories," Levi said.

Jacob's gaze met Levi's. "I don't want anyone to know where I am."

"Why, who are you hiding from?"

"Everyone," Jacob said. "It's a long story."

Levi looked at Terrence, whose gaze was fixed on Jacob. Then Levi looked at Jacob again. "We have all night to listen, so why don't you start by telling us why you're going to Phoenix?"

Jacob licked his lips. "I have a cousin there; he's twenty and lives on his own. I'm hoping I can stay with him."

"Hoping?" Levi said. "He doesn't know you're coming?"

Jacob shook his head. "If I told him, he might phone the cops and tell them where I am."

"Why would the police care where you are?" Terrence asked.

Jacob looked at Terrence. "Because I ran away from foster care; I couldn't stand it there any longer."

"I don't get it," Levi said. "Why are you in foster care?"

"My mom and stepdad are alcoholics. Neither one of them has a job; we live in Section Eight housing." Jacob pointed to the scar on his shoulder. "About a month ago, my stepdad attacked me with a table knife while he was drunk, and that's when Child Services took me away."

"What's wrong with foster care?" Levi said.

Jacob grimaced and shook his head. "I share a room with two boys older and bigger than me. After lights-out, they make me do nasty stuff with them—if you know what I mean. I complained to my foster parents, but they wouldn't believe me, so I ran away and I'm *not* going back."

Levi swung his gaze to Terrence, who made a face like he'd just swallowed something bitter.

"You guys aren't going to report me, are you?" Jacob asked while his gaze flitted from Levi to Terrence.

"Of course not," Levi said. "And we'll get you to Phoenix, no problem. You don't have to worry."

Jacob let out his breath while he stared into the pool water.

LEVI LAY ATOP his sleeping bag in his tent; he listened to Terrence breathe while he thought about Taylor. He'd forgone calling her earlier, and then, when she had phoned *him*, right after supper, he hadn't taken her call. He let it go to voice mail, and her message was brief:

"I puked this morning, not long after I woke up. I'm sure it's morning sickness, and I guess I should see an OB-GYN. Call me when you get this, will you?"

But he hadn't called because he didn't know what to say to her. The gravity of the pregnancy and how it would likely derail his future had settled onto him like a leaden blanket. How much did a guy have to pay each week for child support in Florida? How would his parents and siblings react when they learned he had fathered a child? And once the child was born, would he, Levi, be a part of the kid's life? Did he even *want* to be?

Why did life have to be so complicated?

Chapter Eleven

TERRENCE, LEVI, AND Jacob sat at their campsite's picnic table, sharing a breakfast of French toast Levi had prepared on the propane stove. They passed the orange juice jug around, each taking swallows. The sun had risen an hour before and already the day was warming up. In a nearby desert willow, a mourning dove cooed.

"You chattered in your sleep like crazy last night," Levi told Terrence. "You must've woken me up at least three times."

Terrence ran his fingers through his tangled hair. His eyes were still swollen from sleep and he was shirtless. "Sorry. What was I talking about?"

Levi shrugged. "Most of it was gibberish, but at one point, you were talking to your mom; I know that much."

"What did I say to her?"

Levi glanced over at Jacob, then told Terrence, "Why don't you and I discuss that later on today?"

Terrence lowered his gaze and nodded.

"How long will it take us to get to Phoenix?" Jacob asked.

"Ninety minutes at most," Levi said. "We'll drop you at your cousin's, and then we'll be on our way to Los Angeles."

Terrence looked at Levi and shook his head. "I can't believe we'll be in California tonight. Where will we stay this time?"

"At Topanga State Park; it's west of Beverly Hills, very close to the Pacific Ocean and *real* pretty. I camped there in May when I was driving to Florida."

"Cool," Terrence said.

While Terrence washed the breakfast dishes at the bathhouse, Jacob watched Levi roll up the sleeping bags and disassemble the tent. Then the two of them loaded up the van for departure.

"If you stay in Phoenix," Levi asked Jacob, "will you go to school there?"

Jacob shrugged while he toted the cook stove to the van. "I haven't really thought about it. If I tried to enroll, they'd probably call Child Services in Austin, and I don't want *that* to happen. I'll find a job someplace instead. I don't expect my cousin to let me live with him for free."

"Do you know him well?"

"Sort of," Jacob answered while he stowed the cook stove in the van. "We used to spend Christmas with him and his folks every year until Mom married my asshole stepdad. My cousin was older than me, of course, but we always got along. When I was little, he'd take me to a park near their house, to play on the jungle gym. Then, when I got older, he let me play games on his computer."

Levi hefted the sweating cooler from the picnic table. After he'd stowed the cooler in the van, he wiped his hands on his shorts while he studied the cloudless sky. "Looks like it's going to be another hot day. I can't wait to get back to Palo Alto and some cooler weather."

After Jacob plucked a toothbrush from his backpack, he asked Levi, "Could I borrow some toothpaste from you? I forgot to pack any."

Levi nodded just as Terrence approached, carrying the dish tub that was stacked with silverware, Levi's frying pan, and the coffeepot, all clean and glistening. Morning sunlight reflected in Terrence's dark hair.

Levi produced his shaving kit, then told Terrence, "Jacob and I are going to brush our teeth before we leave. Want to join us?"

Moments later, the three stood at sinks in the bathhouse, scrubbing away. Levi studied himself in the wall mirror before him. Again, he pondered whether or not he should shave but decided against it. Who cared if he walked around with several days' worth of stubble? Certainly not Terrence.

Levi stole a glance at Terrence's reflection in the mirror; he studied Terrence's slender physique, his smooth skin, and close-to-androgynous facial features. And it occurred to Levi that Terrence was just about as pretty as Janice or Krystal had been, but in a more masculine way.

Back at the campsite, they took their respective positions in the van. Then they were back on I-10, rolling through the never-ending flatness and brownness of central Arizona. Already the day was heating up; air entering the van through the open windows was warm and dry like heat wafting from a pizza oven. Off in the distance, crusty-looking mountains rose from the desert floor. A freight train a half mile away, towing at least fifty freight and box cars, chugged on tracks that paralleled the highway.

Levi plopped his sunglasses onto his nose; then he turned to Terrence. "How about a little music? It'll help pass the time."

Terrence shrugged and reached for his clarinet case. Once he'd assembled the clarinet, he dampened the reed with his tongue. He played a few scales, then looked over at Levi. "Any requests?"

"Something different; a song I haven't heard before."

Terrence shifted his weight in the car seat while he rocked his head from side to side. Then he said, "I'll play 'What a Wonderful World' by Louis Armstrong. Ever heard it?"

Levi shook his head.

"Armstrong is probably the greatest jazz hero of all time, even more than Charlie Parker. The airport in New Orleans is named after him."

"You're kidding," Levi said.

"I'm not," Terrence said and launched into the tune, which Levi found soothing as notes slid from Terrence's clarinet, rising and falling in a fashion almost hypnotic. For a moment, Levi forgot his own troubles, as well as those of his travel companions. He stared at the asphalt ribbon before him and focused on the music.

When Terrence finished "What a Wonderful World," Jacob clapped in appreciation. "That's sounded great. Play something else."

"All right," Terrence said, "I'll play 'The Bare Necessities' from the Disney movie *The Jungle Book*."

"Cool," Jacob said. "I always loved that movie when I was little."

Terrence played while Levi studied the highway and the land to either side. The terrain they passed was utterly devoid of trees. The only vegetation present was cacti and sagebrush. Off in the distance was another mountain that looked like it had a tooth growing out of its summit. The cloudless sky was a brilliant blue color. Heat waves shimmered over the roadbed. Already Levi's T-shirt was damp in the armpits. Again, he cursed the desert's torpidity.

But the tune Terrence played had a chirpy quality that Levi liked a good deal; it lifted his mood, and then Levi told himself he should listen to more clarinet music in the future. The notes Terrence played floated through the van like butterflies.

When Levi glanced at Jacob's reflection in the rearview mirror, Jacob's gaze was fixed on Terrence with his head cocked to one side.

Levi returned his gaze to the windshield, and when Terrence finished the tune, Levi waited until Jacob ceased clapping before he spoke. He told Jacob, "We'll be in Phoenix within an hour. Give me your cousin's address, and I'll map our route with the GPS on my phone."

"Will do," Jacob said and pawed through a pocket on his backpack until he found what he was looking for: a dog-eared envelope that he passed to Levi.

Levi steered with his knees while he punched in the address, and studied the GPS map that appeared on his phone screen. "Looks like he lives in an area called Maryvale," Levi said to Jacob. "Have you been there before?"

"Nope," Jacob said. "I don't think he's lived there all that long, maybe six months."

"It's halfway between downtown Phoenix and Glendale," Levi said, "and not too far from I-10. We'll find your cousin's place, no *problema.*"

"Does he live alone?" Terrence asked Jacob while Terrence disassembled his clarinet.

"I'm not sure," Jacob said. "I mean, I haven't spoken to him in a while."

"Maybe you should call him since you're almost there," Terrence said. "That way you won't take him completely by surprise."

"I don't want to do that," Jacob said.

"Why not?" Levi asked.

"It'll be harder for him to send me away if he has to do it in person." Levi's gaze met Terrence's.

Levi raised his eyebrows and then gave his attention to the highway.

MARYVALE WAS A section of Phoenix that reminded Levi of the area in Orlando where Terrence had lived: lots of one-story cinder-block houses with weed and dirt yards and beat-up automobiles resting on oil-stained driveways. They passed apartment complexes well past their prime and strip centers where nail salons and martial arts schools operated. Trees growing here and there looked stunted to Levi.

Jacob's cousin's home occupied a dusty corner lot, a one-story frame structure sitting atop concrete piers, with asbestos-shingle siding badly in need of paint. Shingles on the home's pitched roof were crumbled and curling at their edges. A metal mailbox on a wooden post was listing at a forty-five-degree angle. In the home's side yard, a pit bull chained to a plywood doghouse began barking as Levi parked the **Bo Peep** van on the driveway.

Jacob exited the van with his backpack and sleeping bag and climbed a short flight of concrete steps to the front-door landing. Levi watched as Jacob knocked on the rusted door and shoved his hands into the rear pockets of his jeans. Ten seconds passed while Jacob shifted his weight from one leg to his other. He knocked a second time while the pit bull kept barking and pulling its chain taut.

After thirty seconds or so, Jacob left his belongings on the landing and approached Levi's window. "He must be at work. I guess I'll just wait here 'til he gets home."

Levi nodded. Then he jerked a thumb over his shoulder. "You'll get hungry long before then. Make yourself a sandwich before we leave and grab a soda out of the cooler."

Jacob pursed his lips and nodded. "Thanks. I'll do that."

Chapter Twelve

"I WONDER IF we'll ever hear from him," Terrence said while he and Levi cruised through the Sonoran Desert on I-10. They had already left the Valley of the Sun and Phoenix behind them a half hour before. Jagged mountain peaks rose in the distance to either side of them, and saguaro cacti sprouted from the hardpan here and there.

Before departing Jacob's cousin's driveway, they had both scribbled their cell phone numbers on a scrap of paper Jacob put in a hip pocket of his jeans.

"Let us know how things work out," Levi told Jacob.

Jacob nodded and waved as Levi backed the van into the street.

Now, Levi stared through the windshield and shook his head. "Who knows if he'll stay in touch, but I sure wouldn't want to trade places with him. What a nightmare."

Terrence nodded. "Imagine getting stabbed by your own stepfather. And that stuff about the foster home—how awful."

Levi made a face and shook his head. "No kid should have to deal with those sorts of things. If he has any luck—and he's due for some—the situation in Phoenix will work out for him."

The time was close to eleven, and soon the sun would reach its apex in the endless azure expanse of Arizona sky. The van was heating up; both Levi and Terrence shed their shirts.

Terrence grabbed two plastic water bottles from the ice cooler. He handed one to Levi and opened the other for himself. His Adam's apple bobbed as he guzzled cool water. Then he mopped his brow with his discarded T-shirt.

He asked Levi, "How soon before we get to L.A.?"

"About six hours, which means we'll hit rush hour, and that's *not* a good thing, believe me. I-10 and I-405 will be like parking lots, but that's the only decent route to reach Topanga Park. So, we'll just have to deal with it."

Terrence's cell phone rang, and after he answered it, Levi listened while Terrence talked." We just left Phoenix; we're on our way to Los Angeles."

Terrence turned to Levi. "What time do you think we'll reach San Jose tomorrow?"

"Depends on traffic," Levi said. "Maybe mid-afternoon if we're lucky."

"Around three p.m.," Terrence told his caller. "Will you be home then?

"All right then, me too. Bye."

After Terrence rang off, he placed his phone on the dashboard. Then he looked at Levi. "I just thought of something."

"What's that?"

"How will you get from San Jose to Palo Alto? I can't drive you there myself."

Levi rubbed his chin with a knuckle. He hadn't thought about those logistics either. "We'll have to drop my stuff off at Stanford first. Once we get to your boyfriend's house, maybe he can give me a lift to the Caltrain station in San Jose. Think he'll do that?"

"I'm sure he won't mind," Terrence said. "Not after all you've done for me."

Levi dipped his chin and gathered his eyebrows. "I haven't done all that much, really."

"Are you kidding? Think, it's not just that you've driven us across the country, but you taught me how to camp and how to cook a few things. You changed our flat tire—something I never could have done—and you gave me swimming lessons. You introduced me to beer and wine too; I couldn't have *asked* for a better travel companion."

Levi chuckled and pointed a finger at Terrence. "You left out our kiss in Fort Stockton, or have you already forgotten about it?"

Terrence's cheeks colored, but then a smile crept onto his face while he gazed at Levi. "That's one thing I'll *never* forget. You can be sure of that."

Levi chuckled again while he shook his head. "You'd better not tell your boyfriend we smooched, or he won't give me a ride to the train station."

Terrence snickered. "That whole thing is something private between you and me. Hseuh-Yu doesn't need to know about it."

"So you're already keeping secrets from him?"

Terrence arched his eyebrows. "Do you think I *should* tell him you kissed me?"

"No, *idiot*. I was just teasing. If he's the jealous type, it might get him upset."

Terrence slumped in his seat. For several minutes, he stared out his passenger window without saying anything while the wind tossed his dark hair about. Then he told Levi, "The closer we get to California, the more nervous I'm feeling about meeting Hseuh-Yu. What if he doesn't like me?"

Yeah, Levi thought, *what if?* But he told Terrence, "You're a nice guy. And like I said, you're good-looking, so he'd be stupid not to like you."

Terrence didn't say anything. Instead, he chewed a hangnail. They rode in silence for a time, and then Terrence's phone chimed. After Terrence said hello, the caller spoke for two minutes or more while Terrence made a fist and brought his knuckles to his teeth. When he finally spoke his voice trembled.

"Is he going to be okay?"

More talk burst from the caller while Terrence fingered the edge of his phone. When Levi glanced at Terrence, his eyes were glistening.

"I'm sorry I can't be there," Terrence said, and by now his voice sounded like his nose was congested. "I would be if I could."

The conversation continued another few minutes before Terrence said, "All right, Grandma. I'll call you from California tonight to see how things are. If you get the chance, tell Grandpa I love him."

After Terrence rang off, he put his phone in his pocket. Then he stared at the highway like the roadbed was a nightmare.

"Is something wrong?" Levi said.

Terrence nodded, still staring at the highway.

"What is it?"

When Terrence looked at Levi, a fat tear rolled down his cheek.

"My grandpa had a heart attack this morning; he's in the hospital."

"Is he going to be okay?"

Another tear spilled out of Terrence's eye. "They don't know yet. He's not conscious right now. They're running tests, my grandma said. Maybe they'll know something later."

"I'm sorry," Levi said.

"No," Terrence said while he dried his cheeks with the heels of his hands, "*I'm* the one who should be sorry. I ought to be there right now, at the hospital, so my grandma isn't going through this alone. My grandpa had bypass surgery last year—this isn't the first time he's had heart trouble—so I should have known better than to leave Orlando."

Levi didn't know what to say. He tried to imagine how he might feel if he were in Terrence's position but couldn't.

Terrence shook his head while he spoke. "I'm a selfish little shit, running off to California like this. Just when they need me, I'm not there."

"Don't be so tough on yourself," Levi said. "When we left Florida on Thursday, you had no idea this would happen."

Terrence's eyes watered anew. "You don't understand," he said, his voice quivering. "I'm all they have."

Levi opened his mouth to say something, but then Terrence bent at the waist. He rested his elbows on his knees and buried his face in his hands. His shoulders shook while he wailed like a kid whose dog had been run over by a car. His sobs reverberated off the van's metal walls.

Levi flicked on the van's right turn signal. He braked until his speed slowed to a crawl and maneuvered the van onto the highway's shoulder. After he shifted into Park, he scooted to the inside edge of his seat. Then he placed his hand on Terrence's shoulder and squeezed.

"Sh-h-h-h," he whispered. "Things'll be okay."

"I don't know that they will be," Terrence blubbered. "What if he dies? What then?"

Levi patted Terrence's shoulder; it was all he knew to do at the moment. With his free hand, he switched off the van's ignition. When a transfer truck blew past them, the van shook.

Terrence continued to weep and sniffle.

Say something.

"I guess you and your grandpa are pretty close?"

Terrence bobbed his chin. "He's like a father to me. As I told you, he taught me how to play the clarinet. It's because of him that I'm good with music."

Levi sifted his fingers through the hair on the back of Terrence's neck. "I'm sure he's proud of you. If you get that symphony job in San Jose, it'll make him feel wonderful."

Terrence lifted his face from his hands. He looked at Levi, then reached for the handle on the passenger door. "I need to get out—I'm going to get sick."

Terrence scooted out the door. He bent at his waist with his back to Levi and the desert stretching out before him. He made a coughing sound and a torrent of yellowish liquid gushed onto the ground before him.

Levi grabbed a fresh bottle of water from the ice cooler. He clambered out of the van; then stood alongside Terrence. He placed a hand on Terrence's shoulder while Terrence spat on the ground.

"Are you okay?" Levi said.

Terrence spat again and sniffled while he bobbed his chin.

Levi waved the water bottle in front of Terrence's nose. "Drink some of this. It'll get the nasty taste out of your mouth."

Terrence straightened his spine; he wiped his lips with the back of his wrist and drew a deep breath while he gazed into the desert. He drank from the bottle while another transfer truck roared by.

Then he cried, "I *hate* goddamned Arizona and I hate *fucking* Texas. I hate every place we've been since we left Orlando. Why didn't I stay there? Why am I here?"

"Calm down," Levi said. "You've had a great time on this trip; you told me so back in Fort Stockton. And you're making the journey for a perfectly good reason—to start a new life for yourself."

Terrence didn't say anything. He kept staring at the desert like it held solutions to all his problems.

"Is your stomach okay now?" Levi asked.

"I think so."

"Then let's get going. The sooner we reach L.A., the better."

They returned to the van and rode in silence while desert wind rushed through the windows. Terrence stared through the windshield with a blank expression on his face. Perhaps an hour passed before they reached the dusty little town of Quartzsite.

"It's close to noon," Levi said. "Are you hungry?"

Terrence shook his head.

"Well, I am," Levi said. "I'm going to leave the highway and make myself something to eat."

A sign at the Quartzsite town limits featured a pyramid and three camels sculpted from brown metal. Houses in town were squatty and small, built on lots that were little more than dirt and pebbles. The only major structure was a huge tent that must've been the size of three football fields. According to a sign they passed, the tent housed the town's annual gem show, held in January and February.

Levi found a treeless little park with a picnic shelter, a jungle gym, and restrooms. After he lugged the ice cooler and the food box to the shelter, he set about making a turkey sandwich. Terrence visited the restroom and then joined Levi at the shelter's table. The shelter's roof provided shade from the desert's relentless sun, but the air they breathed was hot and dry. Levi guzzled from a soda can while he slathered mustard onto a slice of bread.

"I can make you a cheese sandwich if you'd like," Levi said to Terrence.

Terrence shook his head. "Thanks, but I don't have an appetite right now."

Levi nodded and laid some turkey and provolone cheese on the bread. After he painted another bread slice with mayonnaise, he added a few lettuce leaves to the sandwich to give it some crunch.

Terrence sat with his hands shoved between his knees. He stared into his lap and said, "I'm sorry I got so upset back there. I guess I'm just a big baby."

"You're not a *baby*," Levi said. "If someone in my family had a heart attack, I'd probably bawl my eyes out too. I mean, it's a terrible situation, so it's okay that you cried and puked. They're ways of releasing tension."

Terrence glanced up a Levi while a little smile crept onto his lips. "Thanks for saying that, Levi. You're actually a very nice guy, do you know that?"

"Am I?"

Terrence nodded. "I'm sure most people assume you're tough because you don't ever say much, and also because you're so masculine. But you actually have a soft side."

Levi grunted.

"It's true," Terrence said. "And I'll bet you'd make a good father to that baby if it should ever be born."

Levi grimaced. "Let's just hope it doesn't. Don't get me wrong; I look forward to maybe being a father someday, but not right now."

Terrence reached into the ice cooler. He plucked out a bottle of apple juice and, after unscrewing the cap, took a large gulp. He swallowed then burped. "It's so dry and dusty out here. My throat feels scratchy and so do my eyes. How can people live in such a place?"

Levi shrugged while he took another bite of his sandwich. He watched a Native American man amble past them on the sidewalk. The man wore a plaid shirt, jeans, and boots. His cowboy hat had a feather poking out of the headband.

Levi's phone chimed, and when he looked at the screen it said "Unknown Caller." He gathered his eyebrows in puzzlement but accepted the call.

A voice said, "Is this Levi?"

"Yeah, who's this?"

"Jacob."

Levi looked at Terrence and made a face. "What's going on Jacob?"

"I'm in trouble. My cousin came home for lunch. When I told him about my situation, he said I couldn't stay with him, no way. He has a housemate *and* a girlfriend so there's no room for me. He was calling the cops when I grabbed my stuff and ran out the door."

"Where are you now?"

"At a mini-mart and gas station not far from my cousin's house. The guy behind the counter here let me borrow his phone to call you."

Levi winced. "So...what'll you do next?"

"I don't know *what* to do; that's why I phoned you guys."

"Look," Levi said, "it's probably best you go back to your cousin's and let the authorities handle things. You can't live on the street in Phoenix; you'd starve to death. And when you get back to Austin, tell your social worker what's going on at your foster home; ask to move to another place."

Jacob's voice sounded frantic. "I *won't* go back to foster care, no way. I'd kill myself first."

Shit, thought Levi while he ran his fingers through his hair.

"What's going on?" Terrence asked.

"Hold on for a minute," Levi told Jacob. Then Levi explained the situation to Terrence while Terrence chewed a hangnail.

"We should go back and get him," Terrence said as soon as Levi finished talking.

"What? Are you crazy?"

"I mean it; we can't just leave him there like that."

"But he's not our responsibility. We gave him a ride; that's all. The authorities—"

"They've already screwed Jacob enough. If he's sent back to Austin, they'll just put him in another pervy foster home; you know they will."

Levi rubbed his chin with a knuckle. What to do? If they drove all the way back to Phoenix, it would throw off the schedule he and Terrence had so carefully planned out. They'd be at least one day late in getting to Palo Alto and San Jose. And what would they do with Jacob when they got there?

"Look, I can't have Jacob living with me on campus; it's not allowed. Plus I can't afford to feed him. And what's your boyfriend going to say if you show up with a sixteen-year-old tagging along? Do you think he's going to let Jacob live in his house?"

Terrence shifted his weight on the bench he occupied. "I don't know what Hseuh-Yu would say. Right now, I'm just trying to put myself in Jacob's position. He's probably scared and doesn't know what to do. We have to go back and get him; we owe him that much."

Levi drew a breath and released it while he studied the screen on his phone. As impractical as rescuing Jacob seemed, Levi knew Terrence was right. Returning to Phoenix was the decent thing to do. After a long moment passed, he brought the phone to his lips.

"Ask the guy behind the counter for the store's address. Then wait for us out front. We'll be there in less than two hours."

Chapter Thirteen

THEY FOUND JACOB seated on a sidewalk in front of the mini-mart, under a canopy that stretched from the storefront to the gas pumps. His backpack and sleeping bag rested beside him on the concrete. When he saw the Bo Peep van approach, he leaped to his feet and ran to the driver's door window.

"Hey, guys," he said while his gaze flitted between Levi's and Terrence's. "You don't know how happy I am to see you right now."

Levi pointed a thumb over his shoulder. "Grab your stuff and hop in. We need to get moving."

Moments later, they were back on I-10, doing seventy. The van's engine hummed while Jacob described the scene at his cousin Todd's.

"You'd have thought I had rabies or something. He said, 'Are you out of your fucking mind? I've got no room for you here. You need to go back to Austin—and I mean today—before my girlfriend and my roommate get home.'

"I asked if I could stay just a few days, 'til I found someplace else to live. And he said, 'No, I'm calling the police and maybe *they'll* find a place for you to sleep.' That's when I bolted."

"I don't get it," Terrence said. "I thought you guys were kind of...close."

Jacob shook his head. "That's what *I* thought, but I guess not. People are fine until you need their help, and then they don't even want to know you, right?"

"Not all people are that way," Terrence said. "Otherwise you wouldn't be in this van right now."

Jacob lowered his gaze and nodded.

"Are you hungry?" Levi said while he gazed at Jacob's reflection in the rearview.

Jacob looked up and shook his head. "Remember the sandwich I made this morning? I ate it while I waited at the mini-mart, so I'm good."

The ride through the western reaches of the Valley of the Sun was *déjà vu*-like to Levi, and it seemed like forever before they returned to the Sonoran Desert with its saguaro cacti, sagebrush, and rust-colored hills. By the time they returned to Quartzsite, shadows were getting long and the sun was making its descent toward the jagged hills ahead of them.

Both Jacob and Terrence had dozed off an hour before, and Levi slumped in his seat, feeling bored and agitated. The desert's monotony and the lack of conversation from his companions forced him to think about the situation with Taylor again. He hadn't spoken to her since Friday, back in Houston, and now he wondered whether he should call her. But what would he say?

"How's the baby doing?" No, that would make it sound as if he cared.

"How are you feeling?" No—same problem as the first question. Why ask if it didn't matter to him?

"Thought any more about an abortion?" He'd already tried that one—more than once—with no results, so why try it again?

No, it was best not to communicate at all. That sent the clearest signal to Taylor that he was simply not interested in her or her pregnancy. Maybe if she finally accepted that fact, she would recognize that giving birth to their child would be a mistake and then she'd end things.

What was it Levi's dad had once told him?

"Sometimes silence speaks louder than words."

They crossed into California at Ehrenberg and passed by the town of Blythe. They entered the Mojave Desert, where the saguaro cacti no longer grew, but Joshua trees abounded. The trees looked to Levi like something from an alternative universe with their twisted limbs topped by pom-pom-like foliage. Afternoon sunlight beat upon huge rock formations that thrust skyward from the hardpan. Off in the distance, low hills loomed.

Levi longed to see the Pacific Ocean, to feel its cool breezes and inhale its salty scent, but that would have to wait until tomorrow. He'd already checked on campgrounds near Riverside; there were several with sites available for tent-camping. But that was still two hours away, and they wouldn't get there before dark. The distance between Riverside and San Jose was four hundred miles. At best, they'd face a six-hour drive the next day.

By the time they reached Indio, the time was past 6:30 p.m. and the sun had already disappeared behind the San Bernardino Mountains to the west. When Levi left the interstate, he was surprised to see shrubbery and grass growing on properties that lined the road into town. Towering palm trees were abundant. Levi pulled into a gas station/convenience store, where he parked at the pumps and roused Terrence and Jacob.

"Time to fill the tank," he told Terrence. "Give me twenty bucks. I'll prepay forty inside, right after I grab a leak. You go ahead and pump the gas."

Terrence yawned while he reached for his zippered money bag. He handed Levi a twenty and made a little note on his spiral pad.

In back, Jacob groaned and stretched his limbs. "Where are we?"

"Indio," Levi answered. "We're finally leaving the desert and about to get into some major mountains."

"Cool," Jacob said. "I don't think I've ever seen a real mountain before."

"I haven't either," Terrence said.

"Well, you might not see too much," Levi said as he opened the driver's door. "It's already close to sunset."

"Then hurry up," Terrence said. "It's not every day a guy gets to see his first mountain."

After Levi paid the cashier for the gas, he visited the men's room where he took care of business. Then he washed his face and hands at a sink that hadn't been scrubbed recently. When he looked at his reflection in the wall mirror, his eyes were red-rimmed and a little puffy, and his hair was in tangles after getting tossed about by wind passing through the van all day. After he sniffed an armpit, he made a face and shook his head.

You smell like a barnyard animal.

Back at the van, Jacob and Terrence conversed while Terrence pumped gas into the van's tank. A gentle breeze wafted across the concrete expanse of the station's apron and fluttered Terrence's hair. Jacob stood with his hands shoved into the rear pockets of his jeans and his elbows jutting.

"If either of you guys needs to use a toilet," Levi said, "do it now. We won't be stopping again until we reach Riverside County."

Terrence looked at Levi and crinkled his forehead. "Riverside County, where's that? I thought we were going to L.A."

Levi shook his head. "It's too far to drive tonight. While you were sleeping, I called Topanga Park and canceled our reservation. Riverside County's ninety minutes from here. We'll buy groceries once we're there and find an RV park."

Terrence nodded while he screwed on the van's gas cap.

"I need to pee," Jacob said. "I'll be right back." Then he walked toward the convenience store, swinging his skinny arms.

"While Jacob's gone…," Terrence said as he returned the gas nozzle to the pump he'd used.

"What?"

"Any ideas on what we can do with him, once we get to San Jose?"

Levi pursed his lips and shook his head. "Like I said, he can't stay with me, and I don't think your boyfriend's going to like harboring a runaway. When we get settled in Riverside tonight, I'll do some Internet research on my phone. Maybe social services in San Jose will have a place for him."

Terrence nodded. "You never told me what I said in my sleep last night. You just said I was talking to my mom."

Levi looked away. "Are you sure you want to know?"

"Of *course* I want to know. Why wouldn't I?"

Levi swung his gaze back to Terrence. "Because you were crying and pleading with her to come back to life. You told her you couldn't stand living without her any longer."

Terrence knitted his eyebrows while he lowered his chin and stared at his shoes. "I guess I'm not surprised. My life's been pretty empty since I lost her. I think everybody deserves at least one person they can love— it's a basic need—but I don't have that person anymore."

Terrence brought his gaze back to Levi's.

"Understand?"

AN HOUR AFTER they left Indio, and just after they passed Palm Springs, the interstate ascended toward the San Bernardino and San Jacinto mountain ranges, a steady climb that made Levi's pulse quicken. Jacob knelt on the van's floor, just behind the console, affording himself an unobstructed view out the windshield. In the passenger seat, Terrence squirmed and twisted a lock of his hair around his index finger.

Air rushing through the van was cooler than Levi had felt in months. The jagged peaks they approached were carpeted with foliage.

It seemed to Levi they had entered a universe entirely different from the one they'd dwelt in for the past three days. They had left the desert behind them. No more cacti and sagebrush. No more dust and dryness, and no more cowboy hats. The sun was a fiery eyebrow, descending behind a distant ridge as they rose. Jacob and Terrence each tried to pick out the highest peak they could find in the fading daylight. Their excited chatter filled the van.

Levi felt like he'd stuck plugs in his ears as their altitude increased. The mountains to either side of them were huge and reminded Levi of ocean swells he'd encountered while deep-sea fishing in the Atlantic.

"We're entering the San Gorgonio Pass," Levi said, raising his voice so Jacob and Terrence could hear him over the chug of the van's engine. "This is how the early settlers got to Southern California from the east."

Jacob whistled. "I'd hate to be a mule pulling a wagon up this road."

Levi nodded. "It's too bad we're losing daylight. Up ahead, there's a huge wind farm. There are hundreds of windmills there, making electricity for Los Angeles. It's quite a sight."

Terrence stuck his head out the passenger door window. He craned his neck, looking upward, and then he pulled his head back inside the van. "This is crazy. We're passing between two solid walls of rock. I can't even see the tops of them they're so tall."

Levi flicked on the van's headlights. Up ahead of them, the sky had turned a shade of pale pink. Perhaps ten minutes passed, and then, right after they passed by Cherry Valley, the road began its descent. Levi took the exit at Oak Glen Road and pulled into a shopping plaza with a good-sized supermarket. After he parked, he studied the screen on his cell phone while he searched for potential camping facilities in the area until he found what he was looking for. Then he placed a call to Yucaipa Regional Park, a county facility only fifteen minutes away.

A ranger at Yucaipa seemed friendly enough, but firm. "We have campsites available, but our office closes at nine. If you're not here before then, you can't rent a site."

Levi gave her his name. "We'll be there in half an hour."

LEVI'S PROPANE LANTERN hissed; the lantern's mantles glowed on a picnic table at the campsite he'd rented in Yucaipa Regional Park, a huge facility nestled at the western base of the San Bernardino mountain range. Levi had already pitched his tent and arranged the sleeping bags and pillows for himself and Terrence. He'd purchased ground beef at the supermarket to make burgers for himself and Jacob, while Terrence had bought tempeh he later fashioned into a patty for grilling. A pyramid of charcoal glowed in the grill provided by the park.

All three of them had bathed at the campground's shower house; their hair was damp, and they smelled of soap and shampoo. Their bath towels draped the limb of a Modesto ash tree. Levi whistled a tune while he cut a tomato into slices for the burgers. Bottles of ketchup and mustard rested on the picnic table, along with a bag of barbecue-flavored potato chips and a jar of dill pickles.

Terrence sipped from a can of beer while he watched Levi work. His clarinet rested in his lap. He'd just finished playing a number he hadn't played for Levi before: "The Rainbow Connection" from *The Muppet Movie*, which Levi had actually enjoyed.

Jacob sat alongside Terrence on a picnic table bench and fiddled with the twist tie on a package of hamburger buns while he talked. "I wish I knew how to play an instrument."

"It's not that hard," Terrence said. "But you have to take lessons and practice each day."

Jacob let out his breath. "At my house, there's never *been* any money for lessons, much less for buying an instrument. We're lucky to have food on the table."

"Has your mom ever worked?" Levi asked Jacob.

"When I was younger, yeah. She had a cashier's job at a discount store—the kind where everything costs a dollar or less. But she slipped and fell on the job, then went on disability. That's about the time she met my stepdad, and that's when the drinking started. It's all gone downhill from there."

"Maybe you should call her," Terrence said, "just to let her know you're all right."

Jacob shrugged. "I'm sure my cousin phoned her, right after I bolted back in Phoenix. And besides, I don't even know if she *cares* that I'm okay. I was in foster care for a month and she never once called me there."

Levi shook his head while he cut slices from a sweet onion. The more he learned of Jacob's family life, the more he felt sorry for the kid. What kind of a future could Jacob possibly have? Would he even finish high school? Levi imagined Jacob working a procession of low-end jobs in the years ahead, and Levi's thoughts troubled him. Didn't Jacob deserve something better? Wasn't he entitled to a family that truly cared for him?

"How long before we eat?" Terrence asked Levi.

"Maybe fifteen minutes," Levi answered. "Why?"

"I'm going to call my grandma real quick," Terrence said, and then he ambled down a pathway that led toward a lake.

After Jacob watched Terrence depart, he said to Levi, "Terrence told me about his grandfather's heart attack. It's really sad. Do you think it'll all be okay?"

"That's hard to know," Levi said while he plucked a can of beer from his ice cooler that rested on the picnic table.

"I've never even *met* any of my grandparents," Jacob said. "My real dad's folks live somewhere in Michigan; they never once visited us. And my mom doesn't get along with her parents, so we never saw them either."

Levi explained Terrence's family situation to Jacob. "His grandparents are all he has. I sure hope the old guy makes it."

Ten minutes later, when Terrence returned, a smile played on his lips and his gait had a spring to it. "It looks like my grandpa's okay; he's sitting up and talking. They put something called a 'stent' into an artery that feeds blood to his heart; I guess the artery was clogged. The doctor thinks he'll be fine."

"Well, *that's* good news," Levi said.

Terrence nodded. "I think I need another beer," he said, reaching into the ice cooler. "It's been a crazy day."

Levi chuckled when he thought back to Thursday night, in Alabama, when he'd first handed Terrence a beer at the campground. "Have I turned you into a drinker?"

Terrence looked at Levi and grinned. "I think so. I like the way beer makes me feel; it helps me relax."

"That it does," Levi said. "I'm going to toss these burgers on the grill. They shouldn't take long."

Terrence followed Levi over to the grill. The coals in the grill were a bright orange pyramid. Levi used a stick to spread the coals into a single layer, and then he placed the burgers on the grate with a spatula.

"I guess you've never done this?" he asked Terrence.

Terrence shook his head. "My grandparents don't barbecue."

Right away, fat dripped from the two beef burgers onto the coals, making a hissing sound and generating a bit of smoke that rose into the still night air.

"How long do you cook them?" Terrence asked.

"Maybe five minutes a side. Every grill is different, so you kind of judge by feel. You don't want to undercook your burger, but you don't want to dry it out either. It takes practice."

Terrence took a slug from his beer. He crossed his arms at his chest and shifted his weight from one leg to the other while he watched the burgers bathe in smoke. "I feel so much better now that I know my grandpa's okay. I don't know what I would have done if he'd...you know."

"Well, now you don't have to worry. You can concentrate on San Jose instead."

Terrence nodded. "What time do you think we'll get there tomorrow?"

Levi nudged a burger with the spatula. "Maybe four p.m. if we're lucky with traffic."

Terrence drained his beer and, after he swallowed, wiped his lips with the back of his hand. "I should call Hseuh-Yu before we go to bed, just to let him know when to expect us."

"If you do," Levi said, "ask him about giving me a ride to the Caltrain station, will you?"

Terrence nodded. "I can't believe we'll be there tomorrow. This trip has gone by so fast and so much has happened. I don't even feel like I'm the same person I was last week."

Levi looked at Terrence and raised his eyebrows. "Maybe you're not."

Chapter Fourteen

LEVI AND TERRENCE rose when the sun's first rays appeared over mountaintops to the east. The morning air was cool, still and dry. After they'd rousted Jacob from the van, the three visited the men's bathhouse to use the toilets. Then they downed a hasty breakfast—OJ, cold cereal, and milk—while the coffeepot gurgled on the propane stove. Both Levi and Terrence wore flannel shirts while Jacob wore a hoodie with a skateboard company's logo on the chest.

"You were restless last night," Levi told Terrence.

Terrence pursed his lips and nodded. "I kept waking up, over and over, maybe six or seven times during the night. I guess I'm just keyed up."

"I didn't sleep well either," Jacob said. "Not to complain, but the van's floor has those ribs running all across it. There's no way to avoid them when you're lying down."

By the time they'd washed up after breakfast and loaded up the van, the sun had crested the mountains to the east and the day was warming up. Traffic was already thick on I-10 when they reached it. It took them ninety minutes to reach the I-5 interchange. They crawled northward through rush-hour traffic, moving fifteen miles an hour at best until the snarl loosened at San Fernando. Then they cruised past suburb after suburb, all of them looking alike to Levi.

In the passenger seat, Terrence stared out his window and shook his head. "This city goes on forever, doesn't it? And the traffic we just went through...."

"I told you it's a shit hole," Levi said. "If I never see L.A. again, I'll be fine with it."

After northbound I-5 narrowed to four lanes, they entered the eastern reaches of Los Padres National Forest, where they drove between low mountains studded with vegetation. Levi had been told that the western regions of the park were spectacular, a hiker's true paradise, and he made a mental note to study up on the park once he was back at Stanford.

West of Bakersfield, they left I-5 and drove westward on Route 58, a two-lane asphalt road that rose and fell like a roller coaster, through hills and canyons, all of it rural and sparsely populated. Beyond the road shoulder, the hills they passed were heavily treed. Levi thought the road was one of the prettiest he'd ever traveled on. In the space of ninety minutes, they encountered only two vehicles: a station wagon and a pickup truck. The sky was a brilliant blue and the wind rushing into the van felt cool on Levi's brow.

No one in the van had spoken for over an hour. Behind Levi and seated on the floor, Jacob snored with his back to a wall. Terrence snoozed in the passenger seat; his chin rested on his sternum and his shoulders rocked from side to side whenever the road curved. Levi studied Terrence's visage again. Terrence had not shaved a single time since they'd left Orlando, yet his face was as smooth as a twelve-year-old's.

Route 58 intersected with Highway 101 at the small town of Santa Margarita, and once they reached there, Levi used his phone to locate a city park. The time was close to noon and Levi's stomach was rumbling, so he left the highway and found a shady spot fronting Santa Margarita Lake, with picnic tables and restroom facilities.

Levi shook Terrence's shoulder until his eyelid's fluttered open. "It's time for lunch."

Terrence yawned and stretched his arms over his head. Then he swung his gaze here and there. "How long was I asleep?"

"At least two hours," Levi said, "and you missed a pretty drive."

Terrence puckered one side of his face and shook his head. "After last night's tossing and turning, I guess I needed some rest. Where are we?"

After Levi explained, he turned and tapped the crown of Jacob's head. "Wake up, man."

Jacob's entire body jerked in response. He blinked a time or two while his head swiveled back and forth. "What's going on?"

"We're stopping for lunch," Levi said.

Minutes later, the three of them sat at a picnic table under a shelter. They busied themselves with making lunch, Levi and Jacob preparing ham and cheese sandwiches, Terrence making a peanut butter and jelly sandwich. A nice breeze came off the lake and rustled the branches of a nearby coastal redwood tree. Sunlight reflected in ripples on the lake's surface, where two men in a rowboat fished.

"So," Jacob asked Levi, "how close are we to Palo Alto?"

"About three hours. We're making better time than I thought we would."

Jacob nodded while he laid lettuce leaves on his sandwich. He told Levi, "When you woke me I was dreaming I was already there, in Palo Alto. I was living with a bunch of priests who wore robes and sandals, in some old building with a garden where they grew their own food. I was working in the garden, pulling weeds, but I didn't mind doing it. The priests were really nice."

Terrence looked at Levi and Levi looked at Terrence. Then Terrence said, "Have you given any thought to where you *will* live?"

Jacob looked up at Terrence. He rubbed the tip of his nose with a knuckle. Then he said, "I was hoping I could stay with one of you guys, at least for a while."

Levi cleared his throat. "The university won't allow you to live on campus with me, so that's not an option. Sorry."

Jacob looked at Terrence. "Where will *you* be living?"

Terrence shifted his weight on the bench he shared with Levi. "I'm moving into a friend's house in San Jose."

"Where's that?"

"It's a city southeast of Palo Alto," Levi said. "Ever heard of Silicon Valley?"

Jacob looked at Levi and shook his head.

"It's where a lot of tech companies are located," Levi said, "and a very expensive place to live."

Jacob's gaze met Terrence's. "Do you think I could stay with you and your friend, at least until I find someplace else?"

Terrence lowered his gaze for a second before he returned it to Jacob's. "It wouldn't be possible."

Jacob crinkled his forehead. "Why not? I won't be any trouble, and I could help out with the household chores—cleaning, yard work, or whatever. And once I find a job, I'll help with the rent."

Terrence used a table knife to spread a layer of grape jelly on his sandwich. "You don't understand. My friend's expecting only *me* to move in with him. He wouldn't be happy if I brought you along; it's not what he and I agreed to."

"But maybe if he met me and we told him about my situation, he'd—"

"It's not going to happen," Levi said to Jacob before turning to Terrence. "Go ahead—explain why you're moving to San Jose, and then he'll understand why he can't stay with you."

Terrence gazed at Levi while he rubbed his lips together, then looked at Jacob. "I'm gay," he said, "and my friend is too. We're going to live together as a couple, so it just wouldn't work having you in the house. I'm sorry."

Jacob's cheeks colored while his gaze flitted back and forth between Levi and Terrence. "What am I supposed to do?" His voice quivered. "Where am I supposed to live?"

"Before we leave here," Levi said, "I'll do an Internet search on my phone. There should be a homeless shelter in Palo Alto where you can stay until you figure things out. That's about the best we can do."

Jacob's face closed down, and then he stared into his lap. "I'm screwed. Next thing you know I'll go back in foster care, and then some other guys will make me their punk."

Jacob sniffled a time or two while a tear rolled down his nose.

"My life sucks," he said. "It just *sucks*."

A LIGHT RAIN fell when they reached a runaway shelter on Alma Street in Palo Alto, right around 2:30 p.m. The shelter was a cinder-block two-story structure that looked like a former motel.

Levi curb-parked the van, then turned to Jacob. "I'm going inside to talk with someone about you. We'll see what they say."

Jacob looked like he was about to cry again. He didn't say anything, only nodded.

In the shelter's office, a gray-haired woman, wearing a billowy ankle-length dress and Bakelite bracelets, sat behind a metal desk stacked with file folders.

When Levi entered, her lips parted into a smile. "Can I help you with something?"

Levi jerked his thumb over his shoulder. "I've got a runaway kid out there, age sixteen. His name's Jacob; he's from Texas. We picked him up hitchhiking two days ago, and now he has no place to stay."

After the woman motioned Levi to a chair alongside her desk, she extended her hand. "I'm Lola Francotti, the shelter's director. And you are?"

Levi introduced himself while they shook. Francotti's grip was warm and firm. After Levi sat, he gave a brief description of Jacob's predicament. "He's afraid he'll get sexually assaulted again if he's sent back to foster care in Texas. The law won't let him live with his mother, and his cousin in Phoenix refused to house him. Can you help out?"

Francotti fiddled with a glass paperweight while she spoke. "For the short-term, of course we can—it's what we're here for—but legally he's a ward of the State of Texas. The juvenile court here will likely send him back to Austin. The State of California has enough runaways of its own to take care of."

Levi lowered his gaze and nodded. "It's what I suspected."

"It was awfully nice of you and your friend to help Jacob out like you did. Most people wouldn't have bothered."

"He's a good kid," Levi said. "I don't want him hurt anymore than he has been."

After Francotti reached across her desktop, she patted Levi's forearm. "I know you want the best for him, but there's only so much you can do, and you've already done it. You brought him to a safe place and now it's time for *us* to take over. Understand?"

Levi nodded.

Twenty minutes later, when Levi and Terrence pulled away from the shelter in the van, Levi felt a deep sadness inside him, as though he'd abandoned a puppy by the side of the road.

In the passenger seat, Terrence looked like he might puke again. "I feel terrible," he said.

"I know," Levi said, "but we didn't create this situation. The adults in Jacob's life made a mess of things for him, and then the State of Texas made it worse. None of that's our fault *or* our responsibility."

Terrence rearranged his limbs. "I should have at least asked Hseuh-Yu if Jacob could stay with us for a while."

Levi shook his head. "It'll be hard enough for you and your boyfriend to adjust to living together without Jacob getting into the mix. You have to put yourself and your relationship with this guy first. So don't feel guilty about Jacob—I mean it."

Terrence pursed his lips and bobbed his chin while Levi steered the van onto the Oregon Expressway. They didn't stay on it for long before they exited onto El Camino Real. Rain continued to fall. When they reached campus, Levi drove them through the university's parklike streets while Terrence asked about the structures they passed.

"That's the football stadium," Levi said, "and that's the Graduate School of Business." Then he pointed to another multistoried brick building. "That was my freshman dorm. My roommate was from Mumbai and a real pain in the ass. He studied every night until 2:00 a.m., and never once did anything for fun."

"What's that tall skinny building with the round roof?" Terrence asked, pointing.

"It's Hoover Tower, named after President Herbert Hoover. He was a Stanford graduate. The view from the top is great; you can see the entire campus."

Levi's new dormitory was a four-story structure with lots of windows and a gabled, barrel-tile roof. The dorm's parking lot swarmed with activity when Levi parked there. Students and parents toted cardboard boxes from the lot and into the building. Many wore rain jackets and their hair was damp.

Levi visited the dorm office, where he picked up his key and signed the necessary forms for occupancy.

Back at the van, Levi opened the rear doors. "Do you mind giving me a hand unloading?" he asked Terrence, and then the two of them carried boxes into the dorm. Levi's efficiency was on the first floor, which was a blessing, as a crowd of students and parents stood at the elevator doors, waiting their turns to ascend to the building's upper floors.

When they entered Levi's apartment and Levi flicked the lights on, Terrence whistled. "Nice place; I'm jealous."

Levi's gaze traveled here and there. Even though the day was dreary, the room still seemed cheerful. One wall was mostly windows looking into the dorm's courtyard, where a concrete fountain bubbled. Two other walls were plaster and painted a cream color. A door led to a private tiled bath. The oak floors gleamed and the furniture—a love seat, a Barcalounger, a desk and chair, a small dining table with two chairs, and a queen-size bed—all looked fairly new. A galley kitchen with a stove, stainless steel sink, refrigerator, and oak cabinets took up most of another wall.

Levi flopped onto the bed and stared at the ceiling. "Home sweet Stanford; it's so good to be back."

"I can't believe you're getting to live here for *free*," Terrence said.

It took them three more trips to the van before Levi's possessions were all inside the apartment. "I've got more stuff in storage," Levi told Terrence when they'd finished. "My bicycle and my winter clothing, stuff like that, but I can take care of those things later. Let's get you to San Jose."

Before they left, Terrence gave Hseuh-Yu's address to Levi and Levi located the home using the GPS on his phone.

"He lives in an area called Willow Glen, south of downtown," Levi said.

"Ever been there?" Terrence asked.

"Never, but San Jose's a huge city and a lot is happening there with the tech industry and all."

They took Highway 101 South out of Palo Alto, and then Levi steered the van onto Route 85, which took them to I-280. They passed shopping malls, sprawling subdivisions, home improvement stores, and multi-storied office buildings with names of tech companies on their flanks. Traffic was thick; in places, they crawled along at ten miles per hour while Terrence stared out the windshield while twisting his limbs this way and that.

"You seem...antsy," Levi said.

Terrence looked at Levi with a pained expression on his face.

"Wouldn't you be if you were me?"

LEVI STARED OUT a rain-spattered window next to the seat he occupied in a Caltrain car. The tracks passed by the backsides of commercial buildings and warehouses. Levi pondered the events of the past hour and tried to decide how he felt about them.

Willow Glen, it turned out, was an expensive neighborhood of leafy streets and pleasant homes built in the 1950s and 60s with emerald lawns trimmed as neatly as pie slices. Hseuh-Yu's house was Spanish-style with stucco walls, casement windows, and a barrel-tile roof. Rose bushes grew in the well-tended yard, where a blue reflecting ball sat atop a concrete pedestal.

Hseuh-Yu was taller than Levi with a slender build and large hands. He wore dress slacks, a white button-down dress shirt, and leather slip-ons when he greeted Terrence and Levi at the front door. His grip was firm when he shook Levi's hand. His dark eyes gazed into Levi's with an intensity that made Levi feel a bit uncomfortable, as though he were being scrutinized. Hseuh-Yu's cheekbones were craggy, his chin square. His dark hair was parted on one side and a cowlick sprang from the crown of his head like a runaway apostrophe.

Terrence and Hseuh-Yu didn't embrace. They only shook hands while smiling at each other.

When Hseuh-Yu invited them inside, Levi demurred. "I really need to get to the Tamien Caltrain station as soon as I can. The next train to Palo Alto leaves in a half hour."

Hseuh-Yu's car was a black Audi four-door with an engine that purred like a kitten. The seats were leather and smelled new. Terrence rode in the passenger seat while Levi sat in the rear. The cowlick on Hseuh-Yu's head kept bobbing whenever he nodded at something Terrence said.

Terrence babbled about the road trip he and Levi had just completed, describing the various campgrounds, the people they had met, and the sights they'd seen. Hseuh-Yu listened intently, but Levi couldn't tell whether or not Hseuh-Yu was truly interested in the journey, or if he was just being polite.

The drive to the Caltrain station took only ten minutes. When Levi exited the car, so did Terrence, and they stood facing each other on the sidewalk while traffic passed by them on Lick Avenue. A light rain continued to fall.

"Well," said Levi, "I guess this is it."

Terrence nodded. "Thanks for everything you did for me; I don't know if I could have gotten here without your help."

"Hey," Levi said, "it was a good trip for both of us, I think."

Terrence lowered his gaze and shifted his weight from one leg to the other; then he looked at Levi. "Is it okay if I give you a hug goodbye?"

Levi felt a lump form in his throat. "Of course."

Terrence slipped his arms around Levi's waist while Levi wrapped his arms around Terrence's neck. Their hips and sternums touched, and they stood in that position for a good thirty seconds. Terrence's cheek rested against Levi's collarbone. Levi felt the warmth of Terrence's body, inhaled the grassy scent of Terrence's hair. When they finally withdrew from each other, Terrence's eyes glistened and Levi felt a bit weak in the knees.

"Call me sometime, okay?" Terrence said.

"Sure," Levi said. "I'll do that."

But now, in the Caltrain car, as the train rolled through Santa Clara, Levi wondered if he'd ever speak to Terrence again. After all, Terrence had his life with Hseuh-Yu now, while Levi had his studies.

It's probably time to move on, McKane.

Chapter Fifteen

BUT MOVING ON didn't prove so easy for Levi.

In the weeks following his return to Palo Alto, he kept replaying his days spent with Terrence inside his head: the campgrounds where they had stayed, the swimming lessons, Terrence's clarinet concerts, his frantic dreams, and his shyness about undressing in Levi's presence. Of course, the kiss they shared in Fort Stockton was something Levi was still trying to process. And Terrence's breakdown when he learned of his grandfather's heart attack was something that stirred Levi's emotions whenever he recalled it. He had never seen a person so distraught.

As weeks passed, Levi realized he had somehow bonded with Terrence in a way he hadn't with anyone else before. The prolonged periods of time he and Terrence had spent together in the Bo Peep van had forced Levi to both talk and listen. You couldn't avoid eye contact or dodge conversation when you spent twenty-four hours a day with the same person for almost a week, could you? And both Levi and Terrence had let their emotional guards down during the trip—an entirely new experience for Levi. They spoke honestly about their problems and hopes, and also enjoyed some pretty good laughs along the way.

Sullen Sam missed all of that terribly.

On a cool and sunny Thursday in early October, Levi walked across the Stanford campus with a backpack hanging from his shoulders. A light breeze stirred the branches dangling on eucalyptus trees he passed. He was thinking about the stupid Truth-or-Dare game he had played with Terrence. He recalled how Terrence stuck a booger on the tip of Levi's nose and how Levi forced Terrence to wear Levi's boxer shorts on his head. The memory brought a smile to Levi's lips, and then Levi realized that Terrence had never returned possession of the boxers to Levi. Had it been an oversight on Terrence's part, or had Terrence intentionally kept the boxers for his own personal reasons?

Levi pulled his cell phone from his pocket. After he located Terrence's number on the phone's directory, he placed a call.

Terrence answered on the third ring.

Levi said, "It's me, your Bo-Peep buddy."

"Hey, I was starting to think I'd never hear from you."

"Sorry," Levi said while he sat on a bench. "I'm real busy with school right now. How are things in San Jose?"

Levi heard Terrence exhale. "They're...okay, I guess."

"Just okay? What does *that* mean?"

Terrence lowered the volume of his voice. "It would take a while to explain, and I can't do that right now."

Levi crinkled his forehead. Then he realized Terrence's boyfriend might be in the same room with Terrence.

"If you're not busy tonight," Levi said, "why don't you take the train to Palo Alto? I'll fix us dinner, something you're able to eat. We can have a few beers and maybe catch up on things."

"That sounds great," Terrence said, "but first I'll need to ask Hseuh-Yu—hold on."

Two or three minutes passed before Terrence returned to their conversation, and when he did his voice sounded agitated. "Sorry that took so long. So, how will I find your dorm? I don't really remember where it is."

"I'll meet you at the train station next to campus," Levi said. "It's a fifteen-minute walk from here. Call me when you're leaving Willow Glen, and try to get here by six thirty."

"Will do," Terrence said. "And thanks for calling, Levi. Thanks a lot."

THE EVENING HAD turned cool. Levi wore a sweater, blue jeans, and a light jacket. When Terrence's train arrived in Palo Alto, the sun had already set and a few stars twinkled in the eastern sky.

Levi barely recognized Terrence when he approached Levi on the platform. Terrence's hair was cut shorter now, with a little length on top and styled with some sort of hair care product. He wore a leather bomber jacket over a sweater and blue jeans. His suede shoes looked new and expensive. He clutched the handle of his clarinet case in one hand, and a platinum wristwatch gleamed on the wrist of his other hand.

"What's happened to you?" Levi said while they shook. "You look like some guy in a department store advertisement."

Terrence's cheeks colored when his gaze left Levi's. "Hseuh-Yu thinks it's important to look your best at all times. He says image is everything."

They crossed under Highway 82 using the pedestrian tunnel and walked southward through campus, where crickets chirped in the eucalyptus trees and coast redwoods.

"It's so weird," Terrence said, "having this kind of weather in October. Back in Florida, we'd still be wearing shorts and a T-shirt."

Levi nodded. "What happened with the symphony job? Did you get it?"

Terrence frowned and shook his head. "The conductor and the first chair clarinetist auditioned me. Afterward, they said I was pretty good, but they wanted someone with more depth of experience, whatever that means."

"Sounds like bullshit," Levi said.

Terrence shrugged. "I found a gig with a jazz band; we play local clubs and weddings mostly. The money's decent and I don't have to wear a tux when I play. The only bad thing is I'm always working Friday and Saturday nights, so I can't spend those with Hseuh-Yu."

"And how does he feel about that?"

"He's not happy with the situation," Terrence said, "but a job's a job, right?"

Levi nodded while they walked past the arts center, where floodlights illuminated the building's facade and a pair of banners publicizing the center's present exhibit hung like dishrags in the still night air.

Terrence asked how Levi's classes were going, and by the time Levi finished describing his fall studies, they had reached Levi's apartment. Once inside, both shed their jackets. Levi opened two bottles of beer. He and Terrence clicked their bottle necks together before each took a swig.

Out in the hallway, two guys kicked a soccer ball back and forth. Every kick produced a thud-like sound, and occasionally the ball would bang against Levi's door. The students talked about Stanford's upcoming football game against Washington while they kicked away. The noise irritated Levi, but he knew they wouldn't quit playing, even if he asked them to.

Terrence smacked his shiny lips. "I forgot how good cold beer tastes. I haven't had one since our last night on the road."

Levi crinkled his forehead. "Your boyfriend doesn't drink?"

Terrence shook his head while he and Levi sat beside each other on the love seat. The clarinet case rested on the coffee table before them. "Hseuh-Yu thinks time spent consuming alcohol is time wasted, plus it's bad for your health."

Levi grunted. "What kind of things *do* you guys do for fun?"

"Hseuh-Yu has a brother who's married and has kids. A couple of nights a week, we play cards with the brother and his wife: Spades, or Hearts, or sometimes Gin rummy."

Levi looked at his beer bottle while he pondered what Terrence had just told him. Then he looked at Terrence and shook his head. "That sounds like something my *grandparents* would call fun, and it sure doesn't sound like you."

Terrence lowered his gaze while his cheeks colored. "You have to understand—Hseuh-Yu's very conservative. He'd never dream of camping in a tent or playing Truth or Dare."

They sipped from their beers, and then Terrence said, "I'm taking swimming lessons at the YMCA. It's a class for adults, and my instructor says I'm doing really well. I lift weights in the fitness center too; I've gained seven pounds since I started."

"Is your driver's license still suspended?"

Terrence nodded. "But only for two more weeks."

"When you get it back, you'll have to take me for a ride in the Bo Peep van. I know a scenic viewpoint in Marin County we could visit. We can drive across the Golden Gate Bridge; you'll like it."

Terrence cleared his throat while he shifted his weight on the love seat. "Actually, the van's in storage right now."

"What? How come?"

"Hseuh-Yu thought it looked dumpy in his driveway. He's going to buy me something nicer, maybe a Honda or Toyota, just as soon as I get my license back."

Levi shook his head. Then he bolted the rest of his beer. The Bo Peep van had brought Terrence and Levi together—it was part of their personal history—and now it was sitting alone and unused, a fact that *bothered* Levi.

"How about another beer?" he asked Terrence.

"Sure," Terrence said, holding up his nearly empty bottle. "I'm already getting a buzz off this first one."

While Levi fetched new beers from his fridge, he told Terrence, "For our dinner tonight, I'm fixing that vegetarian spaghetti dish I cooked for you when we were on the road. Remember the one with the tempeh?"

"Of course," Terrence answered. "I haven't forgotten a thing about our trip, have you?"

Levi shook his head and then rearranged his limbs while he cleared his throat. "Mind if I ask you something personal?"

"Of course not," Terrence said. "Go ahead."

"When we spoke on the phone, you said things were just okay with you and your boyfriend. Are things not working out between you two?"

Terrence looked at his beer bottle and knitted his eyebrows. "It's not exactly what I expected."

"How so?"

Terrence rocked his head from side to side while he talked. "Hseuh-Yu's a very structured guy—he follows a routine in everything he does—and that includes our sex life. It's the same thing every time, and not too exciting."

"I guess that doesn't satisfy you?"

Terrence puckered one side of his face and shook his head.

"Well, *that's* not good," Levi said.

"No," Terrence said. "It's not."

A half hour later, scents of garlic, onion, and olive oil filled Levi's apartment while he sautéed tempeh in a frying pan. At the dining table, Terrence sliced a tomato for a garden salad he was preparing. By now they had each consumed four beers and Terrence's voice was syrupy when he spoke.

"I want things to work out with Hseuh-Yu," he said; "I really do. He's a nice guy and I think he cares for me. It's just that we're so different from each other. And he's almost twice my age."

Levi cleared his throat. "Can I be honest here?"

Terrence looked up from his slicing. "About what?"

"It seems to me that your boyfriend is running your life. You aren't making any decisions for yourself, about clothes or drinking alcohol or anything else. We talked about this when we were on the road—you have a job and you're an adult. You have a right to make personal choices, and he should respect your decisions. Plus I can't believe you put the Bo Peep van in storage."

Terrence lowered his gaze and nodded. "When Hseuh-Yu's brother drove it away, I wanted to cry. I kept thinking of all the conversations you and I had in the van when we made our trip, plus I saw my first mountain through the Bo Peep's windshield." After Terrence looked at Levi again, he said, "It was sort of a *temple* for us, wasn't it?"

Levi nodded while he opened a can of chopped tomatoes. "We drove three thousand miles in that van, but it never once let us down."

"It sure didn't," Terrence said.

Levi opened a bottle of red wine, the same brand he'd shared with Terrence back in Fort Stockton and they drank it with their meal. The wine enhanced Levi's alcohol buzz. Every time he looked at Terrence, he saw a halo around Terrence's precisely coifed head.

Terrence pulled a gleaming state-of-the-art cell phone from his pocket. "Hseuh-Yu bought me this right after I moved in with him. It does amazing stuff, almost like a laptop computer."

Terrence talked about his life with Hseuh-Yu while Levi examined the cell phone.

"Every weekday morning, he leaves the house at seven fifteen. He always calls me at lunchtime to see how I'm doing. He buys our groceries on his way home from work, maybe twice a week. I do the house cleaning and he does the cooking. Saturdays, we do laundry and work in the yard, unless I'm playing at a wedding or some other daytime event. Sundays, we spend the afternoon at his brother's house. We always have a family dinner there before coming back home."

Levi asked Terrence about the jazz band.

"I'm the youngest member by far. The drummer and bass player are in their sixties, the rest are a little younger. They all call me kiddo, but in a nice way. We rehearse on Monday and Wednesday nights, 'cause most of the guys have full-time jobs doing something else. And we play three or four gigs per week."

"How's the money?"

Terrence shrugged. "Better than what I earned at Disney—it's less hours too—so I can't complain. But hey...."

"What?"

Terrence pointed his fork at Levi's nose. "We're only talking about *my* life. What's going on in yours? How are things with Taylor and the baby?"

Levi looked at the tabletop. He drew a breath, then let it out and looked at Terrence again. "A week ago," he said, "her asshole father phoned me. He knows Taylor is pregnant now, and he knows I'm the father. He said if I don't marry Taylor he'll hire the meanest lawyer in Brevard County to come after me for child support. He also threatened to call my folks and tell them about the whole thing."

Terrence made a face like a siren was blasting in the room. "Have you talked to Taylor about it?"

Levi shook his head. "What good would it do? Now that her parents know, she has even less motivation to get an abortion. She's already almost three months into the pregnancy, so I think she's decided for certain to have the baby, and I believe I'm screwed."

"What'll you do?"

Levi rubbed his jaw with the heel of his hand. "Unless my parents agree to pay child support until I graduate—and I don't think they will— then I'll have to quit school and go back to Brevard County. My dad will give me a job at the garage and I'll go to school part-time at night, probably at Central Florida. Great, huh?"

Terrence started to chew a fingernail, but then he yanked his hand away from his mouth. "I've *got* to stop biting myself." He stared at his fingers. "Hseuh-Yu says it makes my nails look ugly."

Levi shook his head. If fingernails were the biggest problem Levi had to worry about, he'd feel lucky. Instead, his entire life plan was about to implode, and there was little he could do to prevent it from happening.

Once they finished their meal, Terrence insisted on cleaning the kitchen. "It's just like it was when we were on the road. You did the cooking, so I'll do the dishes. Fifty-fifty is only fair. It's the way we do it at Hseuh-Yu's also."

After he'd rolled up the sleeves of his sweater, Terrence filled the kitchen sink with soapy water and washed plates and silverware while Levi watched from the dining table. Levi noticed Terrence's frame had filled out a bit since Levi had last seen him. His shoulders looked more sinewy and his butt cheeks had a curve to them. And Terrence wore better quality clothes now, the kind that flattered his physique in a way his baggy shirts and Bermuda shorts had not.

"I lucked out," Terrence said while he scrubbed a plate: "Hseuh-Yu has a dishwasher in his kitchen; it makes cleaning up so easy, and the dishes come out shiny every time. All I have to do is load and unload the machine."

Levi cleared his throat while he crossed his leg over his knee. "It sounds like a comfortable life over there in San Jose."

After Terrence turned his head to look at Levi, he screwed up one side of his face. "It's not perfect, believe me. But building a life with someone isn't easy. Like Hseuh-Yu says, you have to compromise."

"And what sort of compromising does he do for you?"

Terrence shrugged and talked while he scrubbed another plate. "He buys the kind of foods I can eat, and he cooks meals with my diet in mind. He doesn't insist I eat meat, even though he does."

"Anything else?"

"Not really, but what he does is enough, I suppose."

Levi didn't respond to Terrence's remark because he totally disagreed with Terrence's view.

After Terrence finished washing the last of the pans and silverware, he poured himself another glass of wine. Then he went about assembling his clarinet, seated next to Levi on the love seat.

"I'm going to play a clarinet solo I just learned. It's called 'Stranger on the Shore,' and I really like it."

Terrence wetted his reed and played a few warm-up scales. Then he played the tune, a beautiful number that brought to Levi's mind the Brevard County beaches he so loved. He could almost hear waves slapping the shore and the cry of seabirds as the notes oozed out of the clarinet. For a moment, he even forgot his troubles with Taylor.

"That was great," he told Terrence when the song concluded. "Those people at the symphony were fools not to hire you."

Terrence smiled and kissed Levi's cheek. "Thanks. You're sweet to say so."

Levi felt heat in his face while he lowered his gaze and studied the coffee table's surface. The kiss had taken him by surprise, and he didn't quite know what to think of it.

"What is it?" Terrence said.

Levi looked at Terrence and shrugged. "I'm not used to guys getting affectionate with me."

Terrence lowered his gaze before returning it to Levi's. "Sorry if I offended you. It just seemed like the right way to thank you for the compliment, but I won't do it again if it bothers you."

"No, it's fine but...."

"What?" Terrence asked.

Go on.

"When I called you this afternoon, I was thinking about our first Truth-or-Dare game. Remember it?"

Terrence nodded. "Why?"

"You never gave me back my boxer shorts afterward. Do you still have them?"

Terrence's face reddened while he lowered his gaze. Then he looked at Levi and nodded. "Do you want them back?"

"Not necessarily," Levi said. "If you want to keep them, you can; I wouldn't mind. I'm just curious...."

"About what?"

"Do you ever wear them?"

A little smile crept across Terrence's lips. "About once a week, but not on my head."

Levi chuckled. "Aren't they a little big on you?"

"Yeah, but it doesn't matter. I like wearing them; they remind me of the days we spent together."

"Then keep them," Levi said.

Terrence yawned and raised his wrist to study the dial on his shiny watch. "It's already close to ten. I hope the trains are still running to San Jose."

Levi went to his desk to check the Caltrain schedule on his computer. "Shit," he said, moments later, while he stared at the computer's screen.

"What is it?"

"The last southbound train for today left Palo Alto at seven forty-eight. Why didn't I check that earlier?"

Terrence pulled his cell phone from his pocket. "Guess I'll have to call Hseuh-Yu for a ride home, and he's not going to be happy about it. Weeknights, he's normally in bed by ten thirty."

Levi lowered his chin while he rubbed his lips together. He cleared his throat and felt his pulse quicken when he lifted his gaze to meet Terrence's.

Go ahead, say it.

"Stay here tonight. You can grab a train home in the morning."

Terrence poked the cushion beneath him with a fingertip. "Is this thing a fold-out?"

Levi shook his head. "But my bed's a queen-size; we can both fit on it."

Terrence raised an eyebrow. "You're sure?"

"Of course," Levi said. "We shared a tent so why not a bed? It's no big deal."

While Terrence placed a quick call to his boyfriend, Levi brushed his teeth in his bathroom. He listened to Terrence's end of the phone conversation.

"Because there aren't any more trains running tonight.

"It's not anything *like* that."

Minutes later, after they'd undressed, Levi and Terrence lay in the bed, side-by-side on their backs, Levi in boxer shorts and Terrence wearing a pair of skimpy designer briefs. Glow from a courtyard lamppost filtered into the room through the blinds at Levi's windows.

Terrence interlocked his fingers behind his neck. He drew a breath and let it out. "I don't know why Hseuh-Yu gets so jealous. If he even *sees* me looking at another guy in the supermarket, he gets grouchy. It's like he thinks I'm ready to leave him for someone else."

"*Do* you think about leaving him sometimes?"

"Not really. It's just...."

"What?"

Terrence changed position so that he lay on his side, facing Levi. After he bent an elbow, he rested his jaw against the heel of his hand. "Like you said, he wants to control everything I do. If he had his way, I wouldn't even have my job with the band. He'd rather I stayed home like a housewife."

Levi winced. "Has he actually told you that?"

"A few times, yeah."

"But you wouldn't do that, would you?"

Terrence hissed. "There's no way. I like my job and the guys I work with. Plus I think it's important I contribute to household expenses. I don't want to be a kept boy."

Levi reached for his nightstand to check the screen on his phone. "It's past ten thirty and I have an early class tomorrow. Let's get some sleep."

"Okay," Terrence said. After he turned onto his stomach, he worked his cheek against his pillow. "Thanks for letting me stay, and thanks for inviting me over. It's nice spending time with you again."

"I feel the same," Levi said.

LEVI WOKE TO the sound of whimpering. Terrence's back was turned to Levi, and he was shaking so hard the bedsprings squeaked. Levi checked his phone again; the time was close to 3:00 a.m.

Levi shook Terrence's shoulder a few times, trying to be gentle. "Hey, wake up."

Terrence's entire body jerked. Then he flipped over to face Levi. The glow from the courtyard lamppost reflected in tears painting Terrence's cheeks.

"What is it?" Terrence said.

"You were having a bad dream, I guess."

Terrence sniffled while he wiped the tears off his face with his hand. "I was crying, wasn't I?"

"Yeah, and you were trembling like crazy. In fact, you're *still* trembling. What's wrong?"

"I'm sorry," Terrence said in a quivery voice. "I shouldn't have disturbed your sleep, not after you let me stay here."

"It's okay," Levi said. "What were you dreaming about?"

"That just it. I don't know—I wish I did—but could I ask you a favor?"

"Sure."

"When this happens at Hseuh-Yu's house, I turn on my side so I'm facing away from him, and he holds me spoon-style 'til I fall asleep. It helps a lot."

"Then turn over," Levi said.

After Terrence did, Levi scooted toward Terence. Levi's chest met Terrence's shoulder blades and Levi's hips pressed against Terrence's behind. Levi draped an arm across Terrence's chest. He felt Terrence's heartbeat, listened to Terrence's breathing, savored the warmth of Terrence's skin.

And then something extraordinary happened.

An emotional tidal wave washed over Levi, unlike anything he'd felt before. He heard a roaring in his ears while his belly did flip-flops and his heart chugged. His eyes itched, his windpipe flexed, and for a moment he thought he might weep.

Terrence, he realized, meant more to him than anyone else in the world.

"This is nice," Terrence said.

Go on: do it.

Levi's hand trembled when he reached between Terrence's thighs. He gave Terrence a gentle squeeze. Then he left his hand where it was.

Within seconds, Terrence grew as hard as a peg. In the darkness, Levi heard Terrence moisten his lips.

"Do you want me, Levi?"

Levi drew a breath, let it out. "I have ever since we kissed at Fort Stockton, but I'm an Asperger's kid so it took me a while to figure things out. I hope that's okay with you."

Terrence didn't say anything; instead he pressed his lips to Levi's wrist.

Chapter Sixteen

ON A RAINY Tuesday afternoon in mid-November, Levi ducked into a storefront café on University Avenue. He craved a bagel and a cup of coffee. The place was nearly empty. Levi placed his order at the counter, and after he'd received his purchases he took them to a table by the front window. He fished a book of poems by Lawrence Ferlinghetti from his rain-splattered backpack; he was about to open the book when the door to the kitchen swung open and Jacob Fournier entered the room.

Jacob wore a food-stained apron over a long-sleeve T-shirt and blue jeans. He carried a corn broom and dustpan and commenced sweeping the cafe's wooden floor. His appearance hadn't changed since Levi had last seen him, back in August, but now he wore a headband created from a red bandana, and Levi was reminded of photos he'd seen of San Francisco hippies, taken back in the 1960s.

When Levi spoke Jacob's name, Jacob looked up with a quizzical expression on his face, and then his lips folded back into a smile when his gaze met Levi's. He set his broom aside and approached Levi, swinging his gangly arms while his sneakers slapped the floor.

Levi rose from his chair and the two shook hands.

"I didn't know you were still in Palo Alto," Levi said.

Jacob nodded. "I split the runaway center before they could ship me back to Austin. I lived homelessly and panhandled for a little while until I met this street preacher. He let me live at his mission a few weeks until I found this job." Jacob pointed at the ceiling. "Now I live in an apartment upstairs. I share it with the cook and his girlfriend—we split the rent three ways—and it's not bad, really. Plus I get paid under the table, strictly cash, so the law can't trace me here."

Levi nodded. "Are you in touch with your mom?"

Jacob puckered one side of his face and shook his head. "I don't want anyone in Texas to know where I am, not 'til I'm eighteen. I'm not going back to foster care."

Levi saw the wisdom in Jacob's thinking.

Jacob glanced toward the kitchen door and then returned his gaze to Levi. "Have you seen Terrence?"

"A few times," Levi said.

"How did things work out with him and his boyfriend?"

Levi wasn't sure how to answer. Since Terrence's first visit to Levi's campus apartment, Levi had hosted Terrence for dinner and sex twice more. They had also spent a Sunday afternoon exploring downtown San Francisco on foot and by streetcar, causing a major blow-up between Terrence and his boyfriend.

"He told me I was dishonoring him *and* his family," Terrence told Levi over the phone. "Then he wouldn't speak to me for three days, as if I wasn't even there."

Levi thought of Terrence's animated behavior when they had walked the Embarcadero and checked out Fisherman's Wharf. The sun was shining and the air was cool and the sidewalks teemed with tourists. Terrence's head swiveled like a lighthouse beacon while he grinned like a kid on Christmas morning. "I can't believe how cool this place is," he told Levi.

After leaving the Wharf, they walked to the North Beach neighborhood, where Levi introduced Terrence to Levi's favorite place in town: City Lights Bookstore. While they walked between shelves teeming with prose and poetry, Levi explained the store's significance. The words flowed from his lips in a way words normally didn't.

"Back in the 1950s, a movement arose in the US literary community, a rebellion against social conformity and the sexual repressions of the time. The writers were both poets and novelists, and a few essayists too: Ginsberg, Neal Cassidy, William S. Burroughs, Kerouac—guys like that. They called themselves the Beats.

"The movement started in New York City, but it spread to San Francisco, and this place was the epicenter of West Coast Beats culture. All the important Beats poets and fiction writers gave readings here. The store even had its own publishing operation; it gave a lot of up-and-coming writers a chance to be heard."

Terrence pulled at his chin while his gaze traveled about the shelves. "How come Hseuh-Yu never takes me places like this? I doubt he even knows about this bookstore, much less its history. All he reads are technical manuals."

Now, in the Palo Alto café, Levi told Jacob, "Terrence and his boyfriend are having problems right now. I'm not sure their relationship will last."

Jacob glanced toward the kitchen door again while he shifted his weight from one skinny leg to the other. "I need to get back to work, but I'd really like to see you guys sometime. Can we make that happen?"

"Of course," Levi said. "But how do I get in touch with you?"

After Levi handed Jacob a pen, Jacob scribbled on a paper napkin. "The first number's the phone for the café; I'm always here during the day. The second number's the house phone upstairs. I'm usually there at night or, if I'm not, leave me a voice mail. I still have your number in my wallet, so I can call you back."

Levi nodded. "I'll phone you soon, I promise. And look...."

Jacob raised his eyebrows.

Levi said, "I'm glad things worked out for you here."

Jacob gave Levi a little smile.

"DADDY AND I are coming to California," Taylor told Levi on the phone. "The three of us need to meet and discuss things."

Levi sat at his desk and stared out a window into the courtyard, where students with backpacks hanging from their shoulders scurried toward late-afternoon classes. In November, darkness came early in Palo Alto, and Levi's desk lamp was already switched on.

"What things?" Levi said.

"I'm almost into my fifth month," Taylor said. "Decisions have to be made."

"Look," Levi said, "I'm *not* meeting with your father; I've heard all I care to from him. And I'm not sure that a face-to-face meeting between you and me will accomplish much either."

"Levi...."

"What?"

"Let's just talk in person. I'll fly out there with Daddy, but he won't come to our meeting. It'll just be you and me. I don't think it's too much to ask."

Levi drew a breath and let it out while he fingered the edged of his cell phone. *Go on,* he told himself. *I guess you owe her at least that much.*

"All right," Levi said. "When do you want to visit?"

Chapter Seventeen

THE OVEN IN Levi's apartment wasn't large enough to accommodate a turkey, so Levi roasted a five-pound chicken for the Thanksgiving dinner he would serve to Terrence and Jacob. It seemed Hseuh-Yu's family did not celebrate the holiday, so he didn't object when Terrence announced his plan to have the meal at Levi's.

"I'll make a dietary exception since it's a special occasion," Terrence told Levi over the phone when arrangements were made. "I'll eat a little breast meat from the chicken. Now, what should I bring?"

"Give your boyfriend ten bucks so he can buy us a bottle of white wine—Sauvignon blanc to be precise. I'll cover the food, and you should bring your clarinet so we'll have some nice music."

"Will do," Terrence said.

Now, while Levi basted the chicken, he pondered his upcoming meeting with Taylor. She and her father would arrive at SFO in a week, and the meeting at Levi's apartment was set for a day later, after Levi's Friday afternoon classes let out. But Levi had no idea what Taylor's agenda was.

Jacob arrived at Levi's door precisely at 5:00 p.m. In honor of the holiday, he wore a long-sleeve flannel shirt, unbuttoned and untucked, over a T-shirt. His jeans had a rip on one knee, and his ever-present sneakers graced his feet. He wore the same head bandana Levi had seen at the café the last time they'd met. His long hair, as always, was parted in the middle and draped his shoulders. He carried a supermarket bouquet of fresh daisies and ferns wrapped in cellophane, and when he handed them to Levi, he said, "Happy Thanksgiving."

Levi grinned when he accepted the bouquet. "No one's ever given me flowers."

Jacob shrugged. "I thought they'd look nice on the table."

Levi didn't own a vase, so after he'd trimmed the bouquet's stems, he filled an empty mayonnaise jar with water and placed the bouquet in it.

"Are you drinking beer these days?" Levi said. "If so, I'll open two for us."

Jacob shrugged again. "Sure, why not?"

While Levi fetched two bottles of beer, Jacob's gaze traveled about the room. "This is great. Do you live here by yourself?"

Levi nodded while he handed Jacob a beer. Then he sat in his Barcalounger while Jacob plopped onto the love seat.

Jacob grimaced and shook his head. "Must be nice. The apartment I share with Martin and Kaylee isn't much larger than this. I sleep on the sofa while they have the bedroom, and at night I can hear them screwing, even when their door is closed."

Levi rolled his eyes. "But it's better than foster care, right?"

Jacob took a sip of beer. After he swallowed, he said, "Of course, 'cause there's no more...you know. But I'd like to find something better eventually."

A knock sounded on Levi's door, and after Levi hollered, "Come in," Terrence entered, toting his clarinet case and a bottle of wine in a decorative sack. He wore his bomber jacket, a sweater over a button-down shirt, and dress pants that looked fresh from the dry cleaners. His leather loafers were as shiny as mirrors and his hair was carefully styled.

Jacob wolf-whistled while he looked Terrence over. "Looking sharp. Did you win a casino jackpot?"

Terrence's cheeks colored, but a smile crept across his lips. "My boyfriend likes me to dress nicely, so I do it for him. Plus he helps choose my clothes and also pays for them. How can I say no?"

Jacob looked at Levi and narrowed his eyes for a moment and then gazed at Terrence again. "How do you like California so far? Is it what you expected?"

Terrence shrugged while he handed Levi the wine. Then he set his clarinet case on Levi's coffee table. "I can't say I'm all that crazy about San Jose—there's too much traffic and everyone's in a hurry—but I sure like San Francisco. What a cool city."

"I haven't been there," Jacob said. "In fact, I haven't left Palo Alto a single time since we got here in August. I work six days a week, plus I don't have transportation."

After he placed the wine bottle in his fridge, Levi brought Terrence a beer, and Terrence sat alongside Jacob on the love seat. "It smells good in here," he told Levi while he opened the cap on his beer bottle.

"I put lots of garlic and herbs in the stuffing I made for the chicken," Levi told Terrence. "It'll be tasty for sure. We'll eat in about forty-five minutes. In the meantime, why don't you play some music?"

"Yeah, man," Jacob said, "play something special."

Terrence took a swig from his beer and then assembled the pieces of his clarinet while Jacob watched and Levi basted the chicken in the oven. "I'm going to play something you guys probably haven't heard before; it's by George Gershwin. The title is 'Rhapsody in Blue.'"

"Who's George Gershwin?" Jacob asked.

"He was a famous American music composer who was real popular in the 1920s and 1930s," Terrence said. After he wetted his reed and played a few scales, he launched into the number, a jazzy tune with a pitch that rose and fell like a roller coaster. Levi stood in his galley kitchen, tending the food while Jacob remained on the love seat, looking almost hypnotized while he listened to Terrence play. The tune lasted several minutes, and when it concluded, both Jacob and Levi clapped their hands while Levi whistled through his teeth.

Terrence beamed while he reached for his beer.

"How do you remember all those notes?" Jacob asked Terrence.

"Practice is the key," Terrence said. "Lots of practice."

"Do you play for your boyfriend?" Jacob asked.

Terrence shook his head. "He only likes classical music. He has an expensive sound system and he plays mostly Beethoven or Mahler."

Jacob made a face. "Sounds boring."

Terrence rolled his eyes. "Since it's the holiday season, why don't I play a Christmas song my group is rehearsing right now?"

"Which one?" Levi asked.

"'White Christmas,'" Terrence answered. "You guys know that song, right?"

Levi nodded, but Jacob looked puzzled. "Not much music ever got played at our house."

"'White Christmas' was written by Irving Berlin during the Second World War," Terrence told Jacob. "It was the theme song for a Christmas movie made in the 1950s. The version sung by Bing Crosby is the best-selling single record ever produced."

"I never knew that," Levi said.

"It's true," Terrence said. "You can look it up on the Internet."

While Terrence played the tune, Levi closed his eyes and thought of the many Christmases of his childhood, when the McKane household was filled with holiday music. Every year, his parents watched *White Christmas* and *It's a Wonderful Life* on TV in the days leading up to Christmas, and Levi recalled how corny much of the humor in *White Christmas* was, especially Danny Kaye's silly antics.

But Terrence played the tune deftly, changing the volume at times to emphasize certain portions. The notes *oozed* from the clarinet, and when the song ended, Jacob and Levi applauded again.

"Now I think I'm ready for the holidays," Levi said. "We have time for one more beer before we eat. Who wants another?"

Both Jacob and Terrence raised their hands like kids in a classroom. After Levi distributed fresh bottles, he sat in his Barcalounger. He said to Terrence, "Guess who's coming to visit me next Friday."

"Who?"

"Taylor," Levi said, and then he went on to describe his conversation with Taylor, earlier in the week.

"What do you think she wants?" Terrence asked.

"I'm not sure, but I suspect she thinks she can talk me into one thing or another; if not marriage then child support."

A puzzled expression crossed Jacob's face. "I don't understand. Who is Taylor?"

Levi couldn't see any downside to explaining the situation to Jacob, so he did, and after Levi had finished, Jacob shook his head. "You have to support the baby even though you aren't married to this girl?"

Levi nodded.

"That doesn't seem fair to me," Jacob said. "Isn't there something you can do about it?"

Levi studied the bubbles rising in his beer bottle.

LEVI CARVED THE chicken using an electric knife he'd bought at a church thrift shop; the knife hummed as steaming slices of meat peeled away from the chicken's breastbone. He placed the slices on a platter while Terrence poured wine into three juice tumblers. Jacob busied himself with setting the table, placing silverware and paper napkins before the three chairs facing the table. A wireless speaker on Levi's desk played jazz music from a local radio station.

When the platter was stacked high with meat, Levi scooped the stuffing out of the chicken and placed it in a bowl. Then he removed the green bean casserole from his oven. A pleasant mix of scents filled the apartment while each guy filled his plate. Terrence, of course, only took one slice of chicken breast, but Levi appreciated the gesture nonetheless.

They all took chairs at the table, and then Levi raised his juice tumbler while his gaze traveled from Terrence to Jacob and back. "A toast to our journey to California, and to the friendships we formed with one another. And also to these nice flowers Jacob brought and the wine Terrence contributed."

Terrence and Jacob raised their tumblers. Both of them grinned, and then Terrence said, "A toast to Levi for making all this good food, and for bringing us together tonight."

"Yeah," Jacob said, "this is great. It's almost like we're a family. Do you know what I mean?"

Chapter Eighteen

A LIGHT RAIN fell when Levi arrived at his apartment, just after his last class of the week let out. The shoulders of his jacket and the top of his head were damp as he slipped his backpack off his shoulders and tossed it onto his desk. He switched on a floor lamp. After he used the toilet, he studied his visage in the bathroom mirror. He had not shaved in a week and his stubble gave him a rugged look. He ran a brush through his tangled hair. Then he glanced at his wristwatch.

The time was 3:47 p.m., and Taylor was due at four. His gaze traveled first to the bouquet Jacob had brought to Thanksgiving dinner—the flowers still looked somewhat fresh—and then to a framed six-by-four studio portrait of Terrence; it rested on Levi's desk. In the photo, paid for by Hseuh-Yu several weeks before, Terrence wore a sports jacket over a white button-down shirt. His hair was carefully styled, and Levi figured Terrence could have easily passed for a Stanford fraternity boy if he'd wanted to.

Levi opened a can of soda and swished the sweet liquid around in his mouth before he swallowed. He walked to his windows and stared into the dormitory's courtyard, studying water tumbling from the courtyard fountain's tiers. The bark on trees in the courtyard was sodden and as dark as a chocolate bar. The sky beyond the rooftops was the color of dirty dishwater.

Levi shoved his hands into the back pockets of his jeans and shifted his weight from one leg to the other. He fiddled with the edge of a drape and drummed his fingers against a window sill. He watched two boys in crimson Stanford hoodies amble down a sidewalk, both of them smiling and laughing about something one boy had just said. To Levi, they looked like they didn't have a care in the world.

A knock sounded on Levi's door; he flinched when he heard it. After he set the soda can on his kitchen counter, he strode to the door and opened it.

Taylor stood in the hallway, dressed in jeans and a nice pullover sweater. She carried a bulky leather handbag. Her long hair was parted in the middle and she wore makeup. She still looked pretty, but Levi saw a fullness in her face and a bulge in her belly that weren't part of her appearance when Levi had last seen her.

After their gazes met, she tilted her head and made a little smile. "Hello, Levi."

"Hey," Levi said, "come on in." He stepped aside so Taylor could enter. When she passed by, Levi smelled her perfume, a citrusy scent he recalled from their time spent together in Brevard County.

Taylor stood in the center of the room while her gaze traveled from corner to corner. "You live here by yourself?"

Levi nodded. "Would you like something to drink? I have soda and beer. Or I have bottled water too."

"Water's fine," Taylor said, and after Levi brought the water to her, he motioned her to the love seat. Then he sat in his Barcalounger.

He leaned forward, resting his elbows on his knees. "How was your flight?"

Taylor raised a shoulder, let it drop. "We had to go through Denver, and our connection got delayed by weather. The whole trip took almost ten hours."

Levi asked where Taylor and her dad were staying.

"A hotel south of the airport. I drove a rental car down 101 South to see you. Is traffic always that bad here?"

Levi nodded. "Welcome to California: too many people."

Taylor opened the hasp on her purse. "I want to show you something." She handed Levi what looked like a grainy black-and-white photograph with an image in the shape of a lampshade. Inside the lampshade was a fetus; Levi could see the head and nose, a set of fingers, and even a leg.

"That's your son," Taylor said.

Levi didn't say anything; he only studied the lampshade.

"When he comes into this world, he's going to need his daddy, and he'll be a lot happier if both his parents are there for him, especially if all three of them are living under the same roof."

After he placed the sonogram photo on the coffee table, Levi looked up at Taylor. "That's not going to happen."

Taylor raised an eyebrow. "Give me one good reason why not."

"I'll give you several," Levi said. "You've seen this school; it's one of the best in the world. And now you've seen my apartment. I get it all for free because I worked hard and earned my scholarship, so I'm *not* giving it up.

"Then there's another thing: I don't love you. We have nothing in common, and your father and I will never get along. I can only imagine the quarrels we'd all get into."

Taylor rubbed the tip of her nose with a knuckle. "Maybe if you'll give Daddy a chance, you—"

"And there's one more reason—a huge one."

"What's that?" Taylor asked.

Levi rose. After he retrieved the framed photo of Terrence from his desk, he placed it on the coffee table before Taylor.

Taylor's eyebrows knitted while she studied the photo. Then she looked at Levi. "Who's he?"

Levi's pulse raced. His gaze bore into Taylor's while he spoke.

"His name's Terrence; he's my boyfriend. We met three months ago, and I'm not giving him up either."

Taylor brought a hand to her mouth to stifle a laugh, but a giggle escaped from her lips anyway. She shook her head. "You're telling me you're gay?"

Levi shrugged. "I'm not sure what I am." He pointed to the framed photo. "I only know how I feel about him."

"I don't believe it," Taylor said. "What about all the times we—"

"I'm not the same person I was last summer."

After Levi reached for his cell phone, he sent a text message and then looked back at Taylor. "I also talked to a Florida lawyer about our situation. Assuming you can prove I'm the father—and *if* you sue me for child support—Terrence and I will move back to Brevard County so I can work for my dad. If I do that, I'll be legally entitled to joint custody of our child, and that means he'll live with me and Terrence half the time; it's the way things work in Florida."

Taylor squirmed on the love seat while she studied Terrence's photo.

"Ask your lawyer," Levi said. "The fact I have a male partner doesn't preclude me from demanding joint custody if I'm the biological father. I'll be within my rights as a parent, especially if I'm paying child support."

Taylor pointed at Terrence's photo. "What's he like, anyway?"

A smile stole across Levi's lips. "Sweet and smart. He plays clarinet in a jazz band, and he likes to camp. We're a good fit for each other, I think."

"Have you told your parents?"

Levi shook his head. "But I plan to when I fly home for Christmas."

A knock sounded at the door, and when Levi hollered, "Come in," Terrence entered. He was dressed much as he had been at Thanksgiving dinner and carried his clarinet case in one hand. After he placed the case on Levi's desk, he sat on the armrest of the Barcalounger. He draped an arm around Levi's shoulders and kissed Levi's cheek.

"Hey," Terrence said, "how was your day?"

"Good," Levi said, "and getting better now that you're here." He pointed his chin toward Taylor. "I want you to meet someone. Terrence, this is Taylor. Taylor, meet Terrence." Levi looked up at Terrence. "I've been telling her about us, and I guess she's a little surprised. She doesn't believe I could like another guy the way I like you."

"No?" Terrence said, looking at Taylor.

Taylor scowled at Terrence. "I don't know *what* to believe right now."

Terrence looked at Levi and winked. "How about a Friday afternoon kiss?"

"Sure," Levi said.

After he slipped a hand behind Terrence's neck, Levi pulled Terrence's face to his. Their lips met and they made smacking sounds while their tongues dueled. The kiss lasted thirty seconds or so while Levi's stubble ground against Terrence's smooth chin. When the slurping ended, Terrence's face was flushed and his eyes gleamed.

He looked at Taylor and said, "Levi's a great kisser, don't you think?"

Taylor's eyebrows gathered while her face turned almost mauve in color. After she snatched the sonogram photo from the coffee table, she stuffed the photo into her purse and jumped to her feet.

"You're a bastard, do you know that?" she said to Levi. "A complete bastard."

Levi stroked the back of Terrence's neck with his fingertips while he gazed at Taylor. "You're not leaving already, are you?"

Taylor pointed to her stomach. "You don't deserve to have this baby in your life," she said to Levi. She pointed at Terrence. "And neither do you." Then she looked at Levi again. "You'll hear from my lawyer, and I mean *real* soon."

Before Levi could respond, Taylor stormed out the door; she didn't even bother to close it behind her. Levi heard her footsteps as she strode down the hallway. To Levi, the footsteps sounded like gunshots.

Terrence remained seated on the Barcalounger's armrest.

"How'd I do?" he asked Levi.

Chapter Nineteen

ON A SUNDAY afternoon in mid-December, Levi and Terrence occupied the Bo Peep van at Vista Point in Marin County, a spot offering a spectacular view of the Golden Gate Bridge and downtown San Francisco. Terrence sat in the driver's seat. His license revocation had ended and now he could travel anyplace he pleased. The sun shone and a breeze stirred knee-high shrubs growing just beyond the asphalt lot they had parked in. Sunlight reflected in ripples on the bay's surface.

Levi held Terrence's hand.

"We played a Croatian wedding reception last night," Terrence said. "There must have been three hundred people there. You never saw such a party—they even fed *us* dinner—and the booze flowed like water. The father of the bride tipped each of us with one hundred dollar bills."

Levi studied a dark green forest bordering the Presidio, a nonfunctioning Army base on the other side of the bridge. The base was a spot he'd never visited, and he made a mental note to explore the area sometime in the near future, maybe during January. Two days before, Levi had taken his last exam for the semester; his schoolwork was done and now he could relax. Three days hence, he and Terrence would fly to Orlando to spend a week with Levi's family in Merritt Island. Terrence would visit his grandparents on Christmas Eve and again on Christmas Day, at the ALF. Terrence and Levi would also camp for two nights at Bahia Honda Park in the Keys, using Levi's parents' gear.

"You'll love it there," Levi had told Terrence. "The water's as clear as gin. The beach looks like table sugar, and the fishing's good. Plus there aren't any insects in January; it's the perfect time of year for island camping."

Hseuh-Yu had not approved of their travel plans.

"He *exploded* when I told him," Terrence told Levi over the phone, the day after they had booked their flights online. "I said, 'You're not a Christian; you don't celebrate the holiday, so why should you care?' And then Hseuh-Yu said, 'You shouldn't spend an entire week apart from me.'"

Now, in the van at Vista Point, Terrence shook his head. "I'm tired of his possessiveness. When I told him I was spending today with you, he started shouting at me. He said, 'Who's more important, me or Levi? Sunday's supposed to be our family day.' And I said, 'You mean *your* family's day.'" Terrence shook his head again. "Whenever we go to his brother's place, everyone there speaks Chinese. I'm totally ignored; it's like I'm invisible. I don't even know why Hseuh-Yu wants me there."

Levi stared out the windshield as a Navy submarine glided along the bay's surface with a US flag fluttering at its stern. "Can I speak my mind?"

"Sure, go ahead."

Levi turned his gaze to Terrence's while he tightened his grip on Terrence's hand.

"I'm no expert on these matters, but it sounds to me like you and your boyfriend aren't too compatible. I think there's someone else who might...suit you better."

THE DAY BEFORE Terrence and Levi departed for Florida, Levi found a letter in his mailbox from a Melbourne, Florida law firm. It said, in part:

"Assuming you are the biological father of Ms. Bancroft's child, you will be responsible for providing support for the child, once it is born. You will also bear responsibility for all or a portion of the medical expenses associated with prenatal care and delivery of the child. Florida law is clear on these matters. However, Ms. Bancroft is prepared to forgo any claims against you for these expenses—and for future child support—if you will sign a document surrendering any parental rights you might have to the child under Florida law, including but not limited to custody and visitation entitlement."

Levi lifted his chin and gazed at his apartment ceiling.

Hallelujah.

Chapter Twenty

CHRISTMAS DINNER AT the McKane residence took place at noon in the backyard, where a row of picnic tables and folding chairs stood in shade cast by live oaks. The yard overlooked the Indian River and the McKanes' fishing dock. About two dozen family members were there: old folks, toddlers, and every age in between. People ate from paper plates, used plastic silverware, and plastic drinking glasses. The food was served buffet-style; folks dined on ham and turkey and so many side dishes Levi had to go back for a second plate just so he could get a taste of everything.

Terrence sat beside Levi while they ate their meals. The day was sunny but cool. Terrence wore a sweater and blue jeans. He, of course, eschewed eating the ham or turkey, but his plate was piled high with green beans, mashed potatoes, collard greens, and stuffing, all of it smothered in gravy. Sunlight crept through gaps in the live oaks; it dappled Terrence's dark hair.

When Levi's mom passed their table, she paused to rest her hands on Levi's shoulders. She kissed the crown of Levi's head and then kissed Terrence's cheek. "I'm sure glad *both* you boys could be here today. It makes everything just right."

Terrence looked at Levi. Then Levi smiled and winked at Terrence.

Levi's great uncle, a septuagenarian with thinning hair and age spots on the backs of his hands, listened while Levi talked about his and Terrence's cross-country drive, back in August.

"For a guy who'd never camped before," Levi told the old man, "Terrence sure took to it."

The old guy looked at Terrence and spoke with a Florida drawl. "You liked sleeping outdoors, eh?"

Terrence nodded.

The old guy pointed at Levi. "Last time I camped with *him*—he was nine or ten, I guess—he kept farting in the tent; it smelled like a goddamned kennel in there."

Levi and Terrence looked at each other and laughed. Then Terrence said, "He must've outgrown the problem because I never smelled anything."

"Well *that's* good," the old guy said to Terrence Then he swung his gaze to Levi. "And it's good you have a camping buddy out there in California. So many young folks these days won't sleep in a tent or even cook outside."

Levi jerked a thumb in Terrence's direction. "He doesn't just camp; he plays clarinet. You'll hear right after everyone's eaten."

The night before, over Terrence's protest, Levi had insisted that Terrence perform for Levi's family. "It'll be your contribution to the meal. How can you say no?"

They occupied Levi's bedroom, sharing the bed Levi had slept in since he was twelve. An aroma of recent sex scented the air. They lay naked under the bedcovers with the lights switched off. Terrence's cheek rested on Levi's sternum and Levi's arm draped Terrence's shoulder. Moonlight entered the room through a pair of open windows and bathed them in a silvery glow. Beyond the windows, crickets chirped in the live oaks.

Levi stroked Terrence's cheek with a thumb and studied the plaster ceiling while he listened to Terrence breathe. For the first time in his life, he felt utterly comfortable in his own skin.

"I'll play tomorrow if you really want me to," Terrence said.

"I do," Levi said.

Terrence cleared his throat and shifted his weight on the mattress. The springs beneath them squeaked while he spoke. "I talked on the phone with Hseuh-Yu this afternoon, down on your dock. The conversation lasted a long time."

"Do you want to tell me about it?"

Terrence nodded while he licked his lips. "Ever since you and I took the Bo Peep van to Marin County, I've thought about what you said—how Hseuh-Yu and I aren't compatible—and I think you were right—we aren't. No matter how hard I try to make things work, I don't think they ever will. We're just too different, and how am I supposed to fix *that*?"

Levi rubbed his chin against Terrence's scalp. "I don't think you can."

"That's what I told Hseuh-Yu this afternoon."

"So what'll you do now?"

Terrence drew a breath, let it out. "A guy in my jazz band—his name is Keith—owns a house in San Jose, in a neighborhood called Berryessa. Ever heard of it?"

Levi said no.

"It's not as nice as Willow Glen, but it's okay. Keith has a furnished garage apartment; his daughter just moved out of it. At rehearsals last week, he told us he was looking to rent the place if anyone was interested, so I think I'll give him a call tomorrow."

"But I thought you'd never consider living alone," Levi said. "You told me that once, remember?"

Terrence shrugged. "I'm more experienced than I was back then. And I'll ask Jacob if he wants to share the apartment with me. He can help with the rent, and look—we should spend more time with him. I think he needs us right now, don't you?"

Levi nodded because he knew it was true. "It all sounds good."

Terrence rearranged his legs. "I'm sad about Hseuh-Yu, but...."

"What?"

"I'll still have you, right?"

UNDERNEATH THE OAK trees in the McKanes' backyard, Levi rose. He banged a serving spoon against a metal pot until all the folks at the tables quieted and looked in Levi's direction. Then Levi spoke loudly enough so all could hear him.

"My friend Terrence flew here with me from California."

Levi looked at Terrence and said, "Stand up so people will know who you are."

When Terrence rose, his cheeks grew as red as ripe tomatoes. He glanced here and there while shoving his hands into his pants pockets.

Levi continued.

"Terrence is my *best* friend, actually; we drove across the country together in his van last August, and that's how I got to know him. He plays clarinet. Last night, I asked him if he would perform for us today. Like me, he's kind of shy around strangers, but he said he would do it as a favor to me and all of you. So I'm going to ask him to play now."

Terrence assembled the clarinet while folks at the tables watched. He wetted his reed and played a few scales while Levi dragged an empty orange crate to a spot where everyone could see Terrence when he stood on it.

"Here's your stage," he told Terrence, pointing to the crate.

A grin crept across Terrence's face when he climbed atop the crate. He looked across the sea of faces that turned toward him. "I'm Terrence. My grandparents—my mom's folks—are the only family I have, and they stay in assisted living now, so it's really nice to be a part of your family's Christmas. Thanks so much."

Terrence lowered his chin for a moment. He closed his eyes, and a moment later, he opened them and lifted his gaze. "I'm going to play one of my favorite Christmas songs; it's called 'Have Yourself a Merry Little Christmas,' written by Ralph Blane."

Terrence wrapped his lips around the clarinet's mouthpiece. He raised his chin and closed his eyes again. Then his fingers danced on the keypads while notes slid from clarinet's bell. A breeze blew from the river, stirring Spanish moss beards that hung in the limbs of a live oak that towered above Terrence.

To Levi, the song had a melancholy feel to it, as though the composer—when he'd written it—longed for a Christmas past, for a time when he'd been supremely happy like Levi was right now.

Levi studied the faces surrounding him; many belonged to people he'd known all his life. Their gazes focused on Terrence. Even the children present seemed enraptured as the song's notes rose and fell, and when the tune ended, folks applauded; some whistled while others rose to their feet to cheer, Levi among them.

Terrence looked down from the orange crate.

He shined a lazy smile at Levi.

About the Author

Jere' M. Fishback is a former journalist and trial lawyer. He lives on a barrier island on Florida's Gulf Coast.

Website: http://www.jeremfishback.com

Also by Jere' M. Fishback

Tyler Buckspan

Kevin Corrigan and Me

Becoming Andy Hunsinger